Entering
CHRISTMASVILLE

Entering CHRISTMASVILLE

PATRICIA M. BOARDMAN

REIMAGINING HISTORY
FOR TOMORROW

For information contact:
pmboardmanauthor@gmail.com

Published by:
Reimagining History for Tomorrow

Copy Editor: Kim Autrey • Content Editor: Debbie Ihler Rasmussen
Cover design by Maria Levene
Interior book design by Francine Platt, Eden Graphics, Inc.

Paperback ISBN 978-1-958626-09-2
Ebook ISBN 978-1-958626-10-8

Library of Congress Number: Pending

Manufactured in the United States of America

First Edition

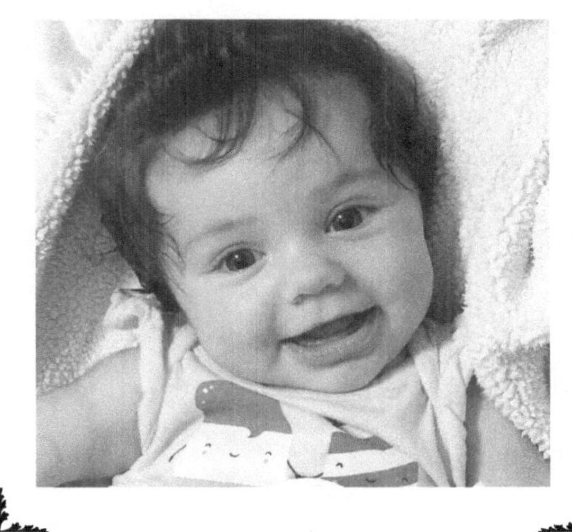

Prologue

WE ALL SEE THEM from time to time. Driving on a country highway, a gravel road, or encapsuled in a metropolitan area. Reminders from our past. Segments of an old highway. Sidewalks and steps that lead to nowhere and foundations of homes long gone. Most of these places where once prosperous little communities where people farmed or milled products at the turn of the last century.

I chose to write a series of stories that are about Ghost Town Christmases. The first is set in Iowa, the second set in a mining town in Utah and the third will be in Southern California. I enjoy history immensely and my imagination will be the vehicle to take us to times and places that hopefully are new to you or which you enjoy visiting.

In 1970 I first saw little Elkport, Iowa. Just a handful of buildings. One block of asphalt was the most these towns ever became. There is almost always a bank, a blacksmith, general store and of course a church and a cemetery. A church is always prominently built on the highest point to remind the citizenry that God is above us all. To remind us to look up when we are burdened with strife.

I always loved the little pioneer church there. So, striking and stalwart looking. I'm always a fan of a belfry. The bell in these communities was a way to communicate, to mourn and to celebrate. The peal of a bell is a language that all in the community understood.

I remember when my sister and I walked up to the church. While we were looking it over, some congregants arrived and started setting up for an event in the basement. We complimented them on the charms of the little pioneer church and asked if we might enter to see the inside. You can't help but wonder of the early sacrifices that were made by farmers to build such an edifice.

Everyone was very kind to us, and they took us down to the basement to show us the event they were planning. We told them our ancestors were from here and that we were walking through all the cemeteries to try to find them. There was a decrepit cemetery next to the church buried in weeds and grapevines 5–6 feet tall. It was difficult to read any of the stones. We were afraid our journey might be fruitless.

Walking around the meandering valley that the Turkey River runs through, my sister Krissy and I wished we could travel in time to see what it was like in the old days when our ancestor John Schweikert was alive. I hope you find this novel, completely an invention and a slice of truth, a holiday favorite.

Most novels are about fictional places. The main town Elkton is completely fictional. I do mention some of the little communities including Dubuque, so I can share what they are really like in brevity. However, this *is not the history of Elkport*, but a fictional story to honor these tiny farm towns. I also wanted to share some parts of history that are less known, as with Black Hawk.

A writer works long and hard to think of a way to tell a tale. We all feel this humility about the process. Even when it feels just right, we always start to doubt ourselves and hope that we entertain and inform you. Ultimately, you as the reader decide what you like or what you don't. I hope you will enjoy my story.

Sincerely,

Patricia M. Boardman

Chapter One

N ETTIE HOLMES gently removed the lid of her brick kiln. Hungry red flames devoured small branches, eventually igniting larger logs, slowly turning them into glowing coals.

Brushing a strand of grey hair away from her face, her wrinkled hands skillfully maneuvered the metal tool over the greenware. Her meticulous attention to detail of this special piece would soon produce a porcelain rendering of a Victorian church.

She wiggled her hands into the heavy leather gloves and lowered the piece into a fiery rebirth. Once the heat had removed the carbon, it will be ready for paint.

Next, she retrieved the completed pieces of a nativity set. Taking the lid off the kiln, she gently began placing each piece inside.

"Hello?"

Startled, Nettie dropped the last piece of greenware onto the concrete floor.

"I'm sorry, I didn't mean to scare you. I was told you needed help—with leaf raking?"

Nettie sighed. "And you are?"

"North Keller, ma'am."

"Come around to the patio." Nettie stared at the broken piece of greenware.

North walked around to meet her. "Let me get that for you."

"No, it's all right." She bent to pick up the pieces but gasped and grabbed her chest. *That still hurts.*

"Are you okay?"

"Yes, yes, I'm fine. Could you wait inside? I'll be right there."

"Okay." He hesitated, and then nodded and walked away.

Nettie studied the two halves of the broken baby Jesus.

Patience, patience is a virtue. It was just an accident.

She had learned patience over years of being alone.

She carefully placed the damaged piece into the kiln and put the lid on. "Maybe I can glue it," she said out loud.

She returned to her desk to find North studying her family photos, but when she came into the room, he immediately said, "I couldn't help but notice what a nice kiln you have."

"Yes," she paused, "this is the last time I'll use it. There's a time and season for everything. This season is nearly over for me."

"That's sad," he looked around at her work, "you're such a talented artist."

"Thank you. This is the last set I'm doing, then I've reached my goal."

North looked thoughtful. "I also work with a kiln."

Nettie smiled. "Porcelain?"

"No, I'm taking a class in Dubuque. My mentor is teaching me how to paint on stained glass. They must be baked as well."

"I can't wait to see your work." She leaned toward North. "Come closer so I can get a better look at cha."

He shyly moved closer, stepping into the natural light. "Is something wrong?"

"No, no. I apologize for my rudeness. It's just that you remind me of someone. Did you say your last name is Keller?"

"Yes."

She sighed. "I guess it's just a coincidence."

He shrugged. "Is the piece that broke part of a set?"

"Yes, it goes with the church."

He glanced around the room. "You have *several* copies of the church."

She nodded slowly. "I haven't decided just what to do with them all. Maybe gifts for fundraisers."

"The detail is amazing. I can't wait to see them painted. That is, if I'm still around." His attention turned to her wall, looking at one photo. "I love the portrait of this couple. It has such a distinct look. We have one like that at our house. I understand they used to take a photograph and then hire a charcoal artist to go over it."

"Early touch-ups I suppose."

"Yes."

"I'm lucky to have it. I borrowed the original to take to a photographer who made a copy, and then I returned it to the owner. The next year, her house burned down. What are the odds?"

"Wow."

The two stared at the photo for a few seconds, then North said, "I'd like to start that leaf raking today. It's going to be close to freezing before we know it."

"Yes, good idea." Nettie pointed to some assorted rakes and a box of lawn bags. He gathered them up, stepped outside, and pulled on the doorknob.

Nettie grabbed the door before it closed. "The roses are ready to be packed, too. Everything you'll need is out there already. I pay ten dollars an hour, is that okay?"

"Yes, ma'am, sounds fine."

Nettie watched him work through the window.

He seems to be a hard worker and knows just what to do. Finally, someone I don't have to babysit.

Chapter Two

M**IKI** L**EWIS** peered out the window of the helicopter at the frozen grey colored skyscrapers. She shivered against the cold windy city of Chicago. Pulling the lapels of her green business jacket closer, she slipped off her spiked heels and wiggled her toes.

The chopper slowly set down on the helipad of the icy roof top. The co-pilot opened the door, and the striking redhead slipped back into her heels and stepped out.

"Miki?" a man called and held open the door to the penthouse.

Miki waved and cautiously hurried to the door, careful to not slip. She quickly stepped inside out of the cold, briskly walking down the hall and into an open door.

"Sorry, I'm late."

Twitchy-faced Mr. Dingle sat at his desk behind his black walnut and brass name plate in his plush office. He impatiently stroked his burly eyebrows.

Miki slipped off her coat, and, once seated in the only empty chair, she again slid her heels off.

Dingle folded his arms. "Let's get started, shall we?"

The meeting participants were seated at a huge circular table. The room had mirrors on every wall with enough inlaid gold trim to require a bank vault.

Mr. Dingle began. "In order to make your town historic, the Main

Street facades have to be returned to their original state, as far as they can be, and then maintained by the buyer."

"Yes," said Miki. "I've been working to find investors to purchase the facades when the actual owner cannot afford to maintain it. I still need two more interested parties."

Mr. Dingle nodded in agreement. "Five have already been acquired, and then we'll wait for spring weather to begin. I've also picked up an adjacent farm to build a subdivision. Franklin Wimmer will oversee that project. I intend to make a bundle on that property. It needs to be thoughtfully developed."

"Right. I'll be making a trip home tomorrow to get some more details worked out," said Miki.

"Get creative, Miki, this must be started by May thirtieth of next year. Otherwise ...."

"Otherwise, it won't even be considered." Miki raised her eyebrows and flashed a confident smile.

A smartly dressed, well-built man in his twenties entered the conference room. Deep blue eyes stared straight ahead from behind dark-rimmed glasses. His chiseled jaw set, he popped up the handle of Miki's suitcase and tucked her small carry-on under one arm.

He turned abruptly and walked out of the room as quickly as he had entered.

Miki hurriedly put her heels on and jumped to her feet. She scowled at Dingle. "I don't need help."

"Oh, you'll find Franklin is really useful." Dingle grinned.

Miki bolted out the door, caught up with the man, and yanked her suitcase away from him. She held out her hand for her carry-on.

The startled man spun around. "Did I do something wrong?"

"When you walk into a room and steal someone's personal belongings, I think that qualifies as wrong."

He scoffed. "Yeah, I've heard what a hot shot you are. Mr. Dingle never stops talking about you."

Miki's eyes widened. "Really?"

"Um, perhaps I could be useful. Mr. Dingle's instructions are that I go with you." He grinned. "I've already rented a car."

Franklin reached for Miki's purse, but she yanked it back as they approached the elevator.

"Sorry, I thought it was small luggage, it's so huge."

Miki scoffed. "Whatever."

"Don't be mad at the boss. He's just a worry wort. Hey, since we have the rental, why don't I just tag along. I'm handy you know; I can push a car out of a ditch in case you drive off the road. Useful."

"Are you implying that because I'm a woman, I'm going to drive off…"

They were distracted by loud commotion when Dingle passed by them with his entourage, impatiently barking orders.

"Doris, I want that contract on my desk by noon!" Dingle's eye twitched. "Larry!"

A male staffer turned around. "Yes, sir?"

"Not *you*. The other Larry, the girl."

She ran toward Mr. Dingle. "Yes, sir?"

"Call my wife and figure out something for her birthday today; around five hundred dollars."

"Got it."

He turned to Miki and Franklin who had now missed the elevator twice.

"I see you two are getting to know one another. Thought you could use a hand, Miki, he's very useful."

"So, I've heard." She shook her head.

Franklin, who at this point Miki had dubbed the modern Clark Kent, shrugged his shoulders and put his gloves on. The elevator doors opened for a third time, and he pulled the luggage inside.

Now Miki's mind was racing realizing her time with her mother and grandmother in Elkton could be ruined with the addition of Franklin. She followed him into the elevator, and the two faced the closed doors, saying nothing.

Miki slipped off her high heels for a third time today and said quietly, "You know what would be useful? If you were a foot massager."

Franklin turned to face her, rolled his eyes, and turned back to the doors. *Is she serious?*

"What was your name again?" Miki asked.

"Franklin."

"Oh, yeah."

They rode to the tenth floor in silence.

Chapter Three

NORTH KELLER entered the carriage barn. Nettie called it her she-shed.

"All done." He put the rake away but noticed some broken hooks, so he hammered several sets of nails into the wall. He then hung the hoe, axe, and lopping shears on the new nails.

He stepped back to admire his work and mumbled quietly, "There, nice and neat. Gloves are in a box. Seed packets in an empty canning jar."

Nettie was at her computer typing furiously, stopping only to look at photos she had pinned to a bulletin board.

North walked up cautiously, afraid of startling her again.

"Well, I'm all done." Looking over her shoulder, he caught a glimpse of a family tree. "Are you a genealogist?"

"Yes, it's been my hobby since I was fifteen. If there's a cemetery within a hundred miles of here, I've been to it. Of course, things have changed. You can do so much online now. You don't have to travel to places anymore. It's convenient but such a loss. I like to look around and see the other graves in the cemetery. A whole town is there. When I think of the collective knowledge they had between them, I wonder what their lives were like." She suddenly stopped and turned around. "Oh, I'm sorry for rattling on, *you* need to be paid."

Nettie handed him an envelope and noticed the tools hanging neatly from the nails.

"Oh, look at that! You're an organized young man. I like that."

She opened a desk drawer and pulled out a twenty-dollar bill. "Here's an extra twenty for you."

North grinned. "Thanks. I think what you're doing is interesting. I want to learn about my family tree."

"Your surname doesn't ring a bell with me. Where is the Keller name from?"

"Oh, just up the hill at Strawberry Bend. Do you ever help other people find their family?"

"Oh, yes, many through the years. I can't stand to leave a good mystery unsolved. Can you come back tomorrow? For more work? I do have more jobs."

Keller nodded. "Would about ten o'clock work? I'll need to milk in the morning and finish my chores."

"That will be fine."

North's grin widened, and he started out of the shed. "See you then."

"North, what are your grandparents' names?"

North stopped. "Peter and Beatrice Keller."

Nettie jotted down the names. She walked to the window to watch him leave. *I like his company. I'd like to surprise him with his family tree.*

She sat back at her laptop and typed in Peter Keller into the search field. She selected census records 1920, 1910, 1900, 1880, 1870, 1860. She began compiling his pedigree chart and a family group sheet for each generation.

I wonder if his ancestor was in the Civil War. "Absalom Keller, there you are. Ah-ha, Minnesota. If it's the same one." She clicked away as the hours passed.

Nettie downloaded documents and added them to the new Keller family tree.

Finally, she checked for the name in a newspaper from Minnesota.

Oh, no. No.

She read each line uncovering more details.

Nettie put her hand over her mouth and shook her head. She said out loud, "They found him in the Money River; the newspaper says he was a floater…he had twelve children."

She clipped the article from the newspaper, added it to the tree, and clicked the logout button.

The logs in the fireplace were reduced to red glowing coals as darkness prevailed.

Tired now, and with the bad news she had discovered weighing on her mind, Nettie called it a night.

Chapter Four

THE NEXT MORNING, Nettie walked to church and sat next to her daughter. When the service was over, she asked Noel if she would mind some company during the week.

"You?" Noel looked surprised.

"I was thinking about it. We never spend any time together anymore."

"It's true we both keep busy. Are you sure you're up to five whole days with me?"

Nettie laughed. "I think it would do me good to get a fresh perspective."

"All right," agreed Noel.

They stopped by Nettie's place in Elkton at 214 Boxelder Street. Nettie jumped out of the car, and the spry senior ran up the stairs, across the porch, and unlocked the front door. She grabbed her previously packed suitcase from just inside the entryway, and the two were off to Dubuque.

"I always loved this highway," said Noel. "During Drivers Ed, our coach had us drive all the way up passed Durango."

"Is that right? It's a long way to go."

"I love the windy road through all the wooded area. Course, at this time of year, we get to see the bluffs again. I bought a CD of all our favorites."

Noel placed the disk in the slender slot, and the CD disappeared into a musical vortex. A familiar song blasted from the speakers. Nettie joined in. "I can't believe you remember that song, Mom."

"I stay relevant by downloading oldies with modern technology. I do have the original vinyl and a turntable, but I can't take it in the car very well."

They both laughed.

Chapter Five

Miki Lewis and Franklin Wimmer picked up the rental car. Miki studied the contract as they walked to the space where it was parked.

"You know, we really didn't need both of our names on the rental."

"Well, you never know when it will be helpful. Look out, there's black ice," he cautioned.

"I'm fine," she snapped and forged on.

Suddenly, she staggered trying to get her feet firmly on the ice but without much success. Awkwardly standing in the middle of the frozen patch with no safe direction to move, she glared at Franklin.

He stared back at her afraid to say anything, not knowing what her reaction might be. "You look like Bambi!" He chuckled.

He was met with an icy stare, and, in an apparent attempt at self-preservation, he simply looked down at the ground.

"Well? Could you help?" she demanded.

"I'm not sure what you want me to do."

Miki tried to take a step but lost her balance and fell sprawling on the ground. Tears spilled down her cheeks as she crawled off the ice on her hands and knees.

Saying nothing, Franklin left their luggage and walked back into the rental car lobby.

15

He returned with a large bag of salt, cut the corner with a little knife on his key chain, and sprinkled the salt making a path to the car. He put the bag of salt and their suitcases in the trunk and then helped her up. He put his arm around her waist as they walked to the car where he helped her into the driver's seat.

Once inside the car, he leaned over and started the engine. Within minutes, warm air soothed her freezing legs.

Miki gave Franklin a side glance. "Okay, so you can be useful."

She struggled to get her leg from under the steering wheel to the dashboard, and then pulled a bottle of clear fingernail polish from her purse. "I tore my stockings. Could you hold this together, and I will dab some polish on."

Franklin said, "I actually can do *this* part, I have two older sisters."

He reached into his jacket and pulled out a tiny first aid kit. He opened a sanitary wipe, cleaned her knee, then blew on it. He dabbed it with antibiotic gel and then put a Band-Aid over the wound.

Miki stared at him. "You have a first aid kit in your *jacket*?"

Franklin grinned. "I'm a Boy Scout, always prepared."

They both looked up when an old man walking toward them shouted, pounding his fists in the air. "Get a room you wild kids!" Suddenly, he lost his balance and disappeared beneath the view of their windshield. Some onlookers rushed to his rescue.

Franklin and Miki laughed, but then Miki turned her attention back to her stocking, holding it in place while Franklin carefully dabbed the polish on the tear.

She watched as he blew on the polish. The heater was blowing like a furnace, and it was warming up inside the car. Intrigued by his pillow-like lips, her face felt hot. She shrugged, blaming it on the heater.

Abruptly, Franklin sat up. "There."

"Wow. You really are good at that."

He nodded. "It's warming up in here." Franklin's eyes locked with hers. "I...I mean the heater works well, doesn't it?"

Miki fenagled her leg back under the dash.

Franklin took off his glasses and wiped them with the corner of his sleeve.

Miki *really* looked at him for the first time. *He has gorgeous eyes. Why am I so mad at him all the time?*

"Would you like me to drive?"

"No! I'm fine."

Franklin looked down for a second.

Miki said, "You know what? I think you *should* drive. My leg needs a rest."

Franklin opened his door, got out, walked around the car, and opened her door. "Okay then."

Chapter Six

FRANKLIN GLANCED over at Miki. Her head was wedged between the window and the seat, and her mouth and jaw were lax. He chuckled. She *would not be happy about the way she looks right now.*

The road sign indicated fifty-eight miles to Dubuque.

Miki snorted and woke up instantly.

"Did you just snore?" Franklin faked shock.

"No. NO! I was just thinking about something." Miki sat up straight in her seat. She noticed the sign as well. "Oh, Franklin! Pull over. I love this little town. Please, I'd like to drive the rest of the way."

Franklin pulled the car to a stop on the side of the road, and they switched seats.

"There are things I want to show you. Gordy Kilgore used to live here," said Miki.

"Who's that?"

"An old radio host my mom grew up with. They always felt like family when they were in our home. He was known as the 'Voice of the River' for recording old stories about the Mississippi River."

Franklin observed a state historic landmark sign and read out loud, "Apple River Fort, such a pleasant name."

Miki drove down a street and turned right onto a dirt road.

Franklin's eyes widened. A large wooden palisade with parapets on the corners stood directly in front of them. "This is the fort? Wow.

It's like cowboys and Indians. It looks so real, Daniel Boone could walk out."

"Imagine this as the only thing out here in 1832." She pointed to her left. "Right down that hill, Black Hawk and some warriors came up over the bank and surprised the settlers. The Indians were just as surprised to see them. There was a brief skirmish. But it was decided Black Hawk was just out hunting for food for his people. He had been forced to the Iowa side of the river away from Saukanuk, his village in Illinois. Seeing the white men plowing over his ancestors' cemetery was the last straw, and he made plans with other tribes in Wisconsin to take his village back. History remembers it as the Black Hawk War of 1832."

"So, the military helicopter is named for him?"

"Uh-huh."

Back on the highway, Miki said, "Next is Galena. You're going to love this."

Franklin tried to take in the expansive view of the river valley town.

"Beautiful," he breathed, "what a quaint town."

"Imagine this river filled with paddlewheel steamboats. This town turned down money from the feds to improve the downtown. It was called Urban Renewal, so it has maintained its historic integrity."

She turned down main street where storefronts with big wooden doors came into view.

"Our car has turned into a time machine," said Franklin.

Miki pulled into a parking lot cleverly designed as an old storefront to match the rest of the town. She parked the car, and the two walked up the street and into a small convenience store taking them back in time to 1856.

Miki went directly to a cooler filled with Wisconsin cheese curds vacuum sealed in plastic.

"You *have* to try these. I loved them when I was a kid. I'll take some home for Mom and Grandma Nettie, too. C'mon, let's go the bakery."

"Now you're speaking my language." Franklin clapped his hands together and followed Miki out into the street.

When they got inside the warm store, they found a table with two chairs. Miki tore open the bag of cheese curds, pulled one off, and took a bite. It squeaked, and she started to laugh.

Franklin's eyebrows narrowed. "What was that sound?"

"The cheese curds."

"They squeak?" Franklin grabbed one and popped it into his mouth. "Squeaking! This is so weird."

They each ate a couple more.

"A squeak fest! Eek, eek." Miki laughed.

Franklin laughed with her, ignoring the looks from the other two patrons. He stood and peered through the glass case at delectable pastries.

"I love real Danish custard!" The girl behind the counter handed him one, and he took a bite. "This is so delicious. I'm glad we stopped."

Back out on the sidewalk, Miki pointed out the three-story building across the street.

"That's the DeSoto hotel named for the famous explorer. It's made of solid red brick with storefronts on the lower level. On the second floor, they had narrow cast iron balconies on the outside of the windows. The windows were very low to the floor back then."

She continued. "In 1856, on that balcony, Abraham Lincoln gave an electioneering speech for John C. Freemont."

"Wait, you mean the Fremont that has a town named for him near San Francisco Bay?"

"Yeah, one in the same."

"I knew he was a California senator, but I forgot he ran for President." Franklin looked back to the balcony. "So, Lincoln was up there? Wow, I wish I could have heard that speech."

"There is a brochure that says reporters of the time said Lincoln was most thoughtful and logical in his story telling. Lots of women from inside the hotel came out to listen to him. The first time he set eyes on Galena was in 1832. He was a soldier in the Black Hawk War."

"Me-she-kia-kiak," said Franklin.

"Holy cow! That was great! Not perfect but nice try."

"I'm smarter than I look."

They both laughed, and Miki continued. "Anyway, Lincoln thought the war was a joke. He said the most blood he ever saw as a soldier was slapping a mosquito."

Franklin chuckled. "That's actually quite funny."

"Another interesting fact is that Jefferson Davis, the Confederate president, was stationed at a lonely fort in Wisconsin. His job was to patrol up and down the border of the Mississippi River in Iowa. It was the only way to keep white people off the Indian land."

"Makes you wonder if the two ever met when they were young," ventured Franklin.

Miki shrugged. "We should start back."

They stopped at the next intersection where they could see a steep hill on one side of the street. A vertical stairway reached as high as the multilevel buildings.

Miki put her hands on her hips. "Do you recall seeing these steps before?"

"Mmm. Vaguely. I think."

"I'll give you a hint. It was in a movie about baseball."

She prodded him further. "Is this heaven? No, it's Iowa."

"*Field of Dreams*? The scene with the Doc? Oh yeah, his wife likes hats. Blue hats."

"Yeah. I'm impressed."

"I loved that part of the movie and the actor, Burt Lancaster."

They walked back to the car, and Miki pulled back out onto the highway.

"The home of General Grant is on the other side of the river, but unfortunately, we need to keep going. But the next thing is the Mighty Mississippi and Dubuque, where I grew up."

Franklin observed her enthusiasm and smiled.

Miki loved driving the winding hilly road past beautiful limestone bluffs and massive farms. Recent snowfall had created drifts on the barren and frigid landscape dotted with skeletal trees.

But the highway held a risk of black ice once the sun went down, and the melted snow freezes.

"You know, I'm enjoying this trip with you, Miki. You're always so put together, and you're a hard worker. My cousin Dingle really seems to favor you. Of course, if you fail at this task, he will drop you so fast…"

She gave him a side-glance. "You're his nephew, don't you have an inside track?"

"Seriously? I had some ideas about taking the firm in a more traditional way using local talent. Dingle wants to lay off most experienced workers and replace them with minimum wage workers from out of the country. There is a lot of institutional knowledge within our company. I can't hurt people that way."

"What did he say?"

"That it's a great idea, but there's just one problem."

"What was it?"

Franklin laughed. "It's not *his* idea."

"What? You're his family. What a jerk."

"I guess I don't stand up to him the way you do." Franklin rubbed his forehead with his fingers.

"I don't stand up to him, really. I just try to believe in myself. Like right now, I'm terrified. I don't have much time to meet all my goals. I think I've over-extended myself, and I'm worried about embarrassing my mom. She doesn't think too much of my…oh, now what?"

"A detour," Franklin said flatly.

"I used to know all the side roads. My mother would take me on little Sunday rides, but so much has changed. All these new highways and subdivisions. I don't even recognize this turnoff." She grimaced. "How do I get to that road down there? Have you seen any detour signs? I am positive there used to be an exit here."

"New road, maybe?"

"No, I missed it!" Miki slammed on the brakes, and the car fishtailed to a stop when it slid into a snow drift.

Miki tried to rock the car forward and back aggressively, but it didn't budge.

"Man, it seems like you've done that a few times. I guess if you grew up in the Midwest, it's second nature. Being from San Francisco, I wouldn't have any idea. We worry about oil slicks there. Kinda the same thing? Maybe?"

Franklin jumped out. He retrieved the salt from the trunk and sprinkled it in front of the wayward tires. He found some loose branches and put them in front and back of the tires.

They waited for a couple semi-trailer trucks to pass.

"Okay, rock the car backward and forward, and I'll push."

Miki put the car in drive and slammed on the gas throwing a combination of salt and mud all over Franklin. He stepped back attempting to miss the debris but slipped into at least three inches of gooey mud.

On the shoulder of the road now, Miki jumped out of the car. "Oh, my gosh, what happened to you?"

Franklin glowered at her but said nothing.

"I'm so sorry. Just a minute."

Miki lifted the trunk, popped open her suitcase, and pulled out a towel. She reached up to close the trunk as a semi changed lanes, and just when he passed them, splashed Miki with mud and ice.

She gasped as the ice-cold watery mud soaked into her skirt and dripped down her pantyhose into her shoes.

Franklin laughed. "You have a towel in your suitcase?"

"That's all you can say?" She stared at him for a minute, then she burst out laughing, too. "Yes, I always carry a towel with me. It's a... thing."

"A thing?"

"Don't ask."

Twenty minutes later, they crossed the Mississippi River.

"This river is huge. What an amazing bridge. It's not the Golden Gate, but I've never seen a river this wide."

"This wasn't the way I wanted you to see the Mississippi. We'll be back here soon enough and see it proper."

She looked over at Franklin. "Would you call my mother and tell her we are in Dubuque and on our way? She's number one on speed dial on my phone."

"Hi, Mrs. Lewis? My name is Franklin. I'm with Miki. She's driving, so she asked me to call. We ran into a detour—she said we should be there about seven."

Franklin pushed end and dropped her phone on the seat. "She said drive safely."

Miki reached for the radio.

"Oh, I haven't' heard this song forever."

She broke into singing like a hillbilly as the artist tell the story of a young man whose true love lives on a mountain with her protective pappy.

"Do people here actually listen to that?" Franklin asked.

"Of course, they do. It's a good song." Irritated, she changed the station.

"Oh, another one! I love this one too, I never get to hear it."

A banjo and guitar start the intro as a country singer croons about a skunk that crossed the highway in middle of the night without looking for traffic and the pollution that followed.

Franklin rolled his eyes. "Did we cross into Kentucky while I was sleeping?"

"No. Of course not. It's a great song. My mom used to have this K-Tel record. We listened to all these novelty songs when I was a kid. We'd sit on the back porch swing that Dad built and laugh and laugh."

"Seriously? Wow, you must have been so bored in Iowa."

"I beg your pardon?" She pulled a face at him. "Fine. I'll change the station again."

"Oh, yay! I can't wait. Is this one a song about paint drying?"

Miki didn't answer, and Franklin stared at her head as it bobbed to the music.

She's too gorgeous. I knew there had to be a fatal flaw somewhere.

Miki laughed and changed the station again and sang even louder.

With a strum of the guitar and smooth baritone voice comedy ensues. The singer weaves a cowboy tale about a cowgirl who rides a moped into town to faceoff with a gunslinger who killed her daddy.

Franklin covered his face with his hands. "I can't stand this. Is there a rock station out of Chicago?"

"It's too far, there's no signal." She sighed. "I guess I could find something out of Dubuque." She flipped through the stations.

The DJ on the radio said "Hits of the 70's."

"Good," said Franklin, "I'll take it."

He glanced out the window when the headlights flashed on a sign. GUTTENBURG 60 MILES.

They continued north on Highway 52 and passed Durango.

"People passing in the night on a two-lane highway has always freaked me out. It's scary on these narrow, winding roads," said Miki.

She looked over at Franklin; he was sleeping.

The road went up steep hills and then down the other side. She turned the bright lights off and on constantly for oncoming cars.

"It sure is dark out here," Miki mumbled.

She started singing to the rock music of the eighties while Franklin slept for a while.

Her loud singing brought Franklin right out of his sleep, and he sat straight up. He blurted as he read the road sign, "Goottenburg three miles."

"It's Guhttenberg."

Franklin shrugged. "I couldn't care less." He mumbled, slumped down in the seat, and closed his eyes again.

At the next intersection, Miki turned left down a country road.

"This is the last stretch." Miki sighed. "Wow, this road has a name now. That's weird, it was a county road before. I'm afraid of what else I'm going see. Or not see."

"How much farther?" mumbled Franklin.

"Not so far, but we must go slower out here. Besides winding roads, there are so many deer. They don't run away once they're on the road. They just freeze and stare into the car lights. Then you hit them or drive off the road."

Franklin didn't respond.

Miki was getting tired of winding dark roads. On the right, she saw a turn off that seemed familiar, and she slowed down to look.

Franklin woke up. "Where are we?"

She drove a little further down the road, and the headlights revealed a rusty sign hanging upside down on a wooden post. It was riddled with bullet holes.

ENTERING ELKPORT

At the end of the road, a slight rise revealed a beautiful old wooden church, the steeple perfectly visible in the moonlight.

"It's so dark down here." Miki looked around. "Something is wrong. There's not one light."

As the car slowly rolled into the little town, they noticed red eviction notices tacked to almost every door. Each was wrapped in red plastic tape, declaring the town uninhabitable.

Miki sighed, tall weeds everywhere. "What a shame. I wonder what happened? I used to love this place."

The gravel under the tires crunched as they gradually rolled forward.

"I'll have to come back later to take pictures before it's gone. It's spooky." She took a deep breath and blew it through pursed lips. "We used to come here when I was little to visit our great-grandparents. So many happy memories eating lunch at the picnic table by the Turkey River. So peaceful. It makes me sad. Someone used to put wreathes in the church windows."

She turned the car around and headed out of Elkport.

Chapter Seven

NETTIE STROLLED DOWN Main Street of Elkton, mesmerized by the beautiful window displays of Thanksgiving pilgrims, bright orange pumpkins, and vertical cornstalks tied with fall-colored ribbons. All mixed with an array of snowflakes, Christmas trees, and stuffed reindeer.

Nettie felt ten years younger just being amid it all.

Through a store window, Nettie could see children laughing and playing around the Christmas displays. A little girl pressed on a stuffed reindeer's hoof and giggled when its red nose lit up. Their laughter warmed her heart, and she wished she had a great-grandchild to hold.

There's still time. She smiled faintly.

Nettie arrived at the general store where Noel worked part-time. The steps seemed easier tonight. She walked through the door just as the Fed-X delivery man walked out. He stopped to hold the door for her but bumped her purse, and some pedigree charts spilled out onto the sidewalk.

The wind caught the loose papers plastering them against some juniper bushes but only for a few seconds. The next swift breeze sucked the papers from the bushes and sent them flying into the dark cloudless sky.

"Hi, Mrs. Holmes. Merry Christmas."

Nettie looked up to see one of Noel's co-workers. "Same to you dear. Have you seen Noel?" she called.

"Mother, I'm right over here." Noel was standing in the doorway of the store.

"Oh, there you are." Nettie walked toward her.

"Do we know when Miki will be here?" asked Noel. "She was supposed to be here this afternoon."

"A man she is with called to let me know they would be late. They stopped in Galena, then ran into a detour, so maybe seven o'clock."

Nettie continued. "How is her sponsorship program going for Main Street? I can't help but think I might be able to help her. I know some old timers."

"Mom, I know you mean well. I don't want you to get your feelings hurt. People like to do for themselves. Things are always so much more complicated than you think they are."

Nettie looked down feeling like a saddle shoe in the seventies. "Well, in my time when there was a problem, we all pitched in together. That's what family is for."

Noel sighed. "Okay, Mom, but let's just focus on getting Miki here first." Nettie eyed her daughter. "You said 'they'?"

"Yes, she's traveling with a young man from work. He said his name is Franklin. He said Miki took him on a historic mini tour of our farm towns." Nettie scowled. "A *guest*." She sighed. "Noel, I want to ask you something. I have a young man working for me. His name is North Keller. I thought he did a terrific job on my yard, and he asked me to help him with his genealogy. I've been hard at it. He has an ancestor in the Civil War on the Union side. I know he's going to be excited that I found his unit, and I studied up on each battle and…"

Nettie reached into her purse to retrieve the pedigree sheets, but they were gone. Puzzled, she looked around.

"What are you looking for?" asked Noel.

"My papers, my pedigree charts. I noticed some curiosities, so I thought I would run it by you. Two heads are better than one."

"Mom, you know the Civil War isn't really my thing." Noel twisted her mouth but then changed the subject. "Do you have that new house done for the Christmas set? It's nearing five o'clock, and our last-minute customers are pouring in. I really don't have time to talk."

Nettie could see what she was talking about. The door kept opening, and more people crowded in.

A nativity scene made of silver and stained glass was attracting a lot of attention. Some of the shoppers pushed the button on the base, and "Oh Little Town of Bethlehem" rang through the store.

In the toy aisle where the kids had congregated was a cacophony of "Here Comes Santa Claus," "Frosty the Snowman," and an occasional squeal of glee.

Nettie answered her daughter. "Oh, yes. It turned out so nice. I carved a wood framed church. I'll bring a couple more in after I paint them." She looked around at the crowd. "I guess I'll see Miki tomorrow. I'm heading home now."

Noel was distracted with customers and didn't hear her mother.

Nettie watched Noel expertly interact with the customers for a few minutes, and then she slowly left the store. She was disappointed not to see Miki, and suddenly felt lonely. Instead of going home, she walked across the street to the coffee shop.

***

"Mom!" Miki burst into the store with Franklin right behind her. Noel grinned. "Hi sweetheart! I'm so happy to see you, Miki!" Several of Miki's friends were among the shoppers and gathered around her, chatting nonstop.

***

From across the street, Nettie watched the commotion. She put her coat on, pulled her hat over her ears, and returned to the store. When she walked in, she went directly to Miki and pulled her from her friends. "Hi, Miki!"

"Grandma!" Miki pulled her grandma into a hug, melting Nettie's heart.

Franklin interrupted. "We've arrived to save your town!"

Everyone stopped talking, stared at Franklin who was still covered in mud.

Miki stammered, "Oh, this is Franklin, my…my colleague from work in Chicago. He's working on converting the Williams' farm into a new subdivision."

Nettie looked Franklin up and down, then mumbled to the people around her, "Well, that explains a lot—he's one of that bunch from Chicago."

The door open, and North walked in carrying two boxes.

He walked directly to Nettie. "Sorry I'm late, Mrs. Holmes. Where should I put these?"

"Oh, North! Thank you! I had forgotten I asked you to bring those." Obviously delighted that he was there she said, "Put them on the glass counter."

She took Miki by the arm. "I would like you to meet someone, Miki, this is my new friend, North Keller. He's very eligible. I mean knowledgeable."

Miki looked sideways at her grandmother. "What?" But she didn't respond to her grandmother's comment.

North's face lit up. "I've heard so much about you. It's nice to meet you."

"Hi." Miki smiled, and they awkwardly stared at each other for a few seconds.

Visibly annoyed, Franklin stepped in front of Miki and said to North, "I would love a tour of your town."

One of the teenagers whispered to her friends, "He's from Chicago."

"Oh, wow." They all giggled.

Unimpressed, Nettie asked Franklin, "Good heavens, what happened to your coat? You're covered in mud. Most embarrassing."

"You're right. Is there a dry cleaner around here?"

"We don't have one. I guess you'll have to buy a new coat or go to Dubuque." Nettie rolled her eyes.

Almost giddy, one of the teenage girls took Franklin's arm and pulled him toward the door.

"We'll show you around." A second girl took his other arm.

Franklin went willingly, but Nettie noticed he kept looking back through the store window obviously trying to monitor Miki.

North backed up slowly, trying to melt into the crowd. Nettie smiled at his shy behavior, but he was unaware of her watchful eye.

Through the window, she caught a glimpse of Franklin's new younger friends overwhelming him with attention as they dragged him down Main Street.

Noel locked up the store, and she, Miki, and Nettie strolled down Main Street. Nettie beckoned for North to join them.

She took his arm. "Oh, by the way, I spent two nights working on your family tree. I brought the sheets with me to show you, but then I lost them."

"Well, that's so nice of you, what a surprise."

"I'll have to reprint them. There are a lot of interesting stories about your family."

"Thank you, Mrs. Holmes."

They joined the others, and they began sizing up the work that needed to be done.

"Oh, this makes my heart ache," said Miki. "I so want to see these wooden exteriors restored to their former glory."

As they walked past the displays of Halloween amid Thanksgiving decorations and Christmas lights, they noticed the names and dates on the buildings.

Franklin's new friends left him, and he caught up with the ladies and North.

Noel pointed across the street. "James Tiller & Sons, 1902. Isn't that one of our surnames, Mother?"

"Yes. Probably related to your great-great-great uncle from England."

"What was his trade?" asked Franklin.

"He owned a wallpaper, paint, and piano store," said Nettie.

"What an odd combination. Was he in charge of all his faculties?" Franklin chuckled.

Nettie grimaced. *This guy rubs me the wrong way.*

"Well," said Nettie flatly, "one was his love, and the other two a way to put bread on the table for a family of ten."

"I see," Franklin mumbled, then he pointed across the street. "I love the fancy design along the roofline of that building."

"Do you mean the blocks that resemble teeth?" asked Nettie.

"Yes."

"They're called dentils. Isn't that funny?"

Franklin's eyes widened. "Dentals? They do look like teeth."

"Den*tils*. It's one of those repeating patterns used under the soffit of a cornice."

"Of course, that sounds familiar now." Franklin seemed to pretend to understand.

North joined in the conversation. "All that detail really sets off the building."

"Could you imagine carving all that by hand?" asked Franklin.

"My dad does that for a hobby," said North, "but he has modern tools, too. Saves a lot of time. He's working on a one-of-a-kind piece right now. It's an antique carving of a baby. It's a lost art."

Noel said, "I'm not into overdone Victorian. Frank Lloyd Wright is my cup of tea. Blending with nature you know, masculine lines."

Nettie pointed up. "Look at the name, North, it's Keller."

"Are they related to me?"

"I have no idea. Maybe a cousin. We'll have to investigate that."

"Ah, I feel another adventure coming on." North rubbed his palms together.

Nettie noticed that North kept glancing at Miki and how distracted he was. She looked over at her granddaughter. Miki flipped her shiny, long auburn hair behind her shoulder, perfectly silhouetting her face in the streetlamp.

That could drive any man crazy.

"North? North?…*North*!" Nettie snapped him back to the conversation. She looked at him quizzically. "I thought you'd be excited."

"I'm definitely excited…uh, what were we talking about?"

"Miki." Nettie chuckled.

He looked surprised and embarrassed. "We were?"

Nettie smiled. *Maybe I can get them together after all.*

North moved ahead from the others, approached a building, and read, "R. L. Schweikert 1898."

Nettie stepped up next to him. "That's my favorite facade."

"It has always attracted me, too," said North.

"They lived near-by in Garber, but they started down in Elkport. Their son moved up here and started specializing in men's clothing. They had belts, suspenders, that kind of thing."

Bewildered, North shook his head. "I don't get it. What was the big deal with suspenders? Old guys always wore them."

"Well, at the turn of the century, they didn't have all the sizes that we have. They just made small and large. The sleeves were all made for the longest arms. So, you wore a garter to hold your shirt sleeve up, and suspenders to hold your pants up. They were so big, they looked like clown pants."

Miki and Franklin had walked up behind them, and Miki said, "I always wondered about that. Barbershop quartets dressed like that."

Miki walked ahead and carefully studied the condition of the next building. "This is the most beautiful building and in the worst shape. Most of the decorative woodwork needs to be completely redone. It will be hard to find an investor for this."

"Was it a bank?" asked Franklin.

"It was, and what a beauty in its day. I used to have an account here. It had a beautiful, pressed copper ceiling under this one." Nettie leaned in to observe the crumbling drywall.

"Looks like it's been vacant awhile. That's scary," said Franklin.

Miki looked up to the second story. "I can picture this as a store with an apartment above."

Noel pulled her coat collar up around her neck. "I'm getting cold."

Miki linked arms with Nettie. "Grandma, can we go over to your house? Do you have your Christmas village up this year?" She turned to Franklin and North. "Oh, you guys have to see it."

Chapter Eight

MIKI PARKED HER CAR in front of her grandmother's house, and everyone climbed out.

"Is this your house, Mrs. Holmes?" Franklin did not wait for an answer. "It's beautiful. Like a San Francisco mansion in miniature."

"Your yard looks great, Mom," said Noel.

"North has been helping me with the leaves. I thought I would get an early start before the winter snow."

Miki looked at Franklin. "If you think this is a miniature mansion, wait till you see the inside."

He lifted his hand palm up. "Ladies first."

Once inside the door, they observed a mountain of red and green bins, and towers of lighted Victorian houses still in their boxes.

Nettie sighed. "It doesn't look like much now. You must give me time to weave my magic."

The furniture in the living room had been cleared and dusted, leaving the surfaces ready for Nettie's Christmas village. Electrical cords were laid out all over the floor, each leading to a power outlet.

North piled cut logs into the fireplace, preparing to light the fire.

Nettie opened a large chest. "I have blankets here for anyone who wants one."

Noel headed for the kitchen. "Is the apple cider in the fridge, Mom?"

Nettie called back, "Yes, dear." She turned to the others. "How many want cider?"

All hands went up. Franklin raised both of his, and they all laughed.

"An extra-large for Franklin, Noel." Nettie was still laughing.

Franklin jumped up and walked into the kitchen, and Nettie followed him.

Noel looked up when they walked in.

"Let me help you with that pot," said Franklin. "It's a heavy tri clad. My mother had this waterless cookware, too." He set it on the stove.

Miki called from the living room, "Grandma, can we help you get the houses out of the boxes? That was my favorite job when I was a kid."

Nettie walked back into the living room, and Miki continued. "We did that the day after Thanksgiving."

Miki picked up the old-fashioned theatre village piece. "Grandma, remember when I wanted to be an actress?"

"Yes, and I said you could have this theatre when you grow up. Every time I get it out, I think of your chubby cheeks."

"Wait, what was that?" Franklin's head poked nearly sideways from the doorway to the kitchen.

Miki rolled her eyes. "Nothing."

Franklin came into the room. "So, you had chubby cheeks?"

"Grandma's exaggerating."

"I doubt that." North chuckled. "What play was it?"

Noel walked back into the room. "Wasn't it *Charlotte's Web*?"

Nettie looked at her daughter. "Yes, she was a rat."

Miki scowled. "I was not a rat. I was an *adorable* mouse. I was Templeton."

"She had the cutest costume and make up," said Noel.

Nettie lifted a photo album from an antique cabinet and flipped the pages. "Here she is."

"Oh, my gosh, you did have chubby cheeks." North laughed.

Miki rolled her eyes and walked toward the kitchen. "Okay, that's enough. Is the cider hot yet?"

"I'll help you," Franklin and North said in unison. They glared at each other.

Noel hurried past them both getting to the kitchen first. Defeated, Franklin and North turned around.

Noel and Miki returned. Noel carrying a tray of cider and Miki a plate of Halloween cookies.

Miki licked her lips. "I love this recipe for Spritz refrigerator cookies. You always made jack-o'-lanterns and ghosts for the trick or treaters and me!"

"You remember that?" asked Nettie.

"Of course, I do, Grandma." Miki took a big bite of cookie.

They gathered around the fire sipping hot cider and crunching on orange and purple cookies.

"I love fall, don't you?" Miki asked anyone who would listen.

Noel wrapped a blanket around her shoulders and sat on the raised hearth. "Mom, when you and North get done decorating here, maybe you could put my wreath on my door, and a string of lights across the top of my porch. Then I'll be done decorating." She grinned.

"Very funny, Noel," said Nettie.

"I like outdoor lights. I'm just not an indoor detail person like you, Mother."

"Well, I love it," said Nettie, "so let's get to it."

The group took the houses out of boxes and carefully placed them on the fireplace and furniture pieces.

"Should we carry these boxes out to the carriage barn, so they're not in your way?" asked North.

"That would be great." Nettie sat down and stretched her tired back.

Miki pulled out bright red tinsel wrapped around a string of red lights. "I'll get the guys to put this up, so you don't have to get on a ladder, Grandma."

"Thank you, Miki."

She plugged them into a socket, and the two men draped the lights evenly over the nails along the ceiling.

Nettie smiled. "That's a huge start. Thank you so much."

Franklin yawned. "We've had a long drive today, and I'm having a hard time keeping my eyes open."

"Me, too," agreed Miki.

"Where are you staying, Franklin?" asked Nettie.

He grabbed his coat. "I'm going to a Bed & Breakfast down the street. Are you ready, Miki?"

"McCullough's? That's a lovely place. Catherine's a wonderful host," said Nettie.

"I'm staying here," said Noel. "I'm heading to bed, Mom." She gave her mom a kiss on the cheek.

North laughed. "I'm going home."

Nettie walked the three to the door and closed it behind them.

I wish they didn't have to leave.

Sadness rushed over her as she peeked through the curtains watching them laugh as they got into Miki's car.

I wish I could get in the car with them.

She walked over to her red miniature dachshund who had been sleeping near the hearth the entire evening.

She patted her head. "I'm lonely already, Gingersnap."

Her dog looked up, seemingly to console her.

"Yes, I do love being with you, too, little girl." She picked her up and snuggled the dog's head under her chin.

A mutual comfort.

Chapter Nine

THE TOWN HALL was packed for the meeting when Miki and Franklin ducked inside and slid into two seats. This was an important meeting, as it would decide the fate of historic Main Street.

Miki scoped the faces in the room. It was painfully obvious to her that not everyone agreed with the new historic Main Street plan.

Miki tried to bring Franklin up to speed.

She pointed to the right side of the hall. Facing them, a stern looking woman sat in a chair holding so tight to the arms it was as though someone was about to abduct her.

"That's the town skeptic, Frances Sniff, she goes by Fanny. It's funny, but my mother asked her when she remarried if she was going to change her first name to Frances? She said good heavens why would I do that? I've always been Fanny. She runs the local library part-time with an iron fist like we are still in the 1940's. It's the quietest room in the state.

"The woman next to her is her cohort, Anita Bath. She runs the only antique store in town and endlessly complains to the town council that 'there isn't enough business and what are they going to do about it?' It's believed that her downturned mouth is a tattoo since it never moves."

Franklin snickered.

"She's worn her frizzy, greasy hair the same way since I was sixteen years old. The same with her glasses. A spinster. Any future investing idea is a waste of money in her opinion. In five years, she'll be an artifact, and we can add to her the museum."

Now Franklin was laughing so hard tears were running down his face. Miki's impish grin made him laugh even more.

Her remarks could be meanness from someone else, but with Mikki? No. Never. She's just turning reality into humor, to keep from being frustrated. Undeterred in her goals.

He watched her dramatic flair, stretching her arms with the grace of a ballerina, then wiggling her hips into the office chair. She settled in, quickly writing on a notepad.

Franklin felt as though he was walking a little taller with a spring in his step.

Miki walked to the front of the room. "Tonight, I wanted to have a brainstorming meeting to get your input. I'm going to write a topic on the chalk board." She turned to the board, her back to the room. "Let's discuss what people would like to see in their town, what services?"

She continued. "We have already discussed the sandwich/bakery concept with live music in the summer months. But there are seven vacant business blocks and several empty lots on Main. What do you think could draw visitors to our town?"

A soft-spoken woman raised her hand. "Ah, a dry cleaner."

"Okay." Miki wrote dry cleaners on the board.

A lanky man wearing overalls jumped up enthusiastically. "We should have one'a them gas station-mini marts."

A bald, overweight man from his chair yelled, "What the heck are you trying to do, bankrupt me, Ted? I have a gas station with a pop and candy machine. And they're all antique."

"Especially the candy! I opened a chocolate bar last week, and it was all white," said Ted.

"It's just some of that white chocolate," growled the bald man.

"Your son said it was old."

"The pop machine's an antique, too," continued the annoyed bald man.

"They haven't made them small bottles for forty years."

"Well, when they start making um again, Ted, I'll fill the machine."

"Sorry. It was just an idea," mumbled Ted, and he sat down.

"Excuse me, uh, for those that don't know me, which is no one, my name is Jeb. I think Charlie should change the name of his grocery store from Piggly Bigly to Humpke's General Store since that's the name on his building, and it seems more historic."

Charlie objected. "My store has been a Piggly Bigly since 1960. That's historic."

Another man said, "Well sure, if you're not very old."

"Okay. Let's not get sidetracked with so much detail right now. We've had some good ideas and some equally good concerns." Miki tried to control the room.

North raised his hand. "How about a museum? There are a lot of old farm implements around the Graham Building. Also, there's an empty lot next to it for some outside displays and maybe room to build a gift shop."

Another man said, "I'm Matt. We could start with the history of the town, from the Native Americans on up to the pioneers. Jack Williams' son studies all those Injun things in college. He's an expert."

"I have my great-grandfather's Civil War uniform."

"That's a great idea, John. We could talk about the businessmen who built the blocks we're restoring."

Miki noticed heads nodding throughout the room.

Nettie stood. "I think it's a great idea, too. And how about some-place to show off our local art. John takes photographs; young North here does stain glass with farm equipment and antique car parts—unique. I make greenware, too, and maybe have a room for classes? Lillie and Roger both do gorgeous renderings of farm scenes. That's very in right now."

"I make quilts," said a stout woman in the back row.

"There you go." Nettie smiled with satisfaction.

"Well, if we're going to have all these items in the museum, then when will they ever get to my antique store. I'll be ignored. I vote 'no' for the gift shop, but for a sign that says go next store to *my* Fanny's Antiques. That only seems fair."

"Now how long is this meeting going to take? I'm Bill, by the way," he growled. "You know in case none of you know my name." He turned and walked out the door calling over his shoulder, "I got milkin' to do in the morning."

Chapter Ten

THE WIND HOWLED outside Nettie's shed as night settled in. Nettie pulled a sweater over her head and wiggled into it.

When she heard the anticipated knock on the door, she immediately opened it to find North holding an envelope in his hand.

"Did you get it?" she asked.

North grinned and handed her the large manila envelope. "Here you go, Mrs. Holmes."

"We're friends now, North, why don't you to call me Nettie."

"Thanks! I will."

Nettie sat at her desk and motioned to North to pull up a chair as she removed the family group sheets and perched North's family information on a book holder.

On her computer, she opened the Family Ancestor site, clicked on search, then Census records. She typed in North's grandfather's name, Peter Keller, then his birthday, 3 September 1919. On the right of the screen, a list of names and census records popped up.

"Your grandfather was born in 1919. I'm going to look at the 1920 Census." She clicked again and like magic it popped up. "There he is. His father's name was Wolfgang. He was born about 1897. Look here, oh, we lucked out. See this name on the bottom?"

"Karl Keller?"

"Yes, notice his age?"

"Forty-five. Is that my great-great-grandfather?"

"It sure is." Nettie smiled.

North's eyes widened. "Wow."

"Let's check the 1880 census for Karl Keller." Nettie clicked the keyboard. "There he is. Karl's father is…"

"Klaus? This is so exciting. I can't wait to tell my family." North leaned closer to the screen. "And by the date and year of the census, he was born about 1852, right?" He didn't wait for an answer. "So, could he have been in the Civil War? No, what am I saying? He was only nine years old when the war broke out."

Nettie pointed at the screen. "There's his street address on the left, his wife is Gertude. Here's their ages and where they were born."

North picked up a family group sheet and studied it. "It's Granny, wow, she was one year old. I can't imagine her that young. Look, Grandpa Keller is further down the page. He farmed a hundred and sixty acres."

"Times were very difficult during the depression," said Nettie. "Sometimes the dairy farmers had to pour milk out on the ground because they couldn't make enough selling it."

"Dad said he had to sell some of the land to pay the bills to keep our house. We rented out rooms, and Grandma Keller cooked for the men."

"I see your great-grandfather was in WWI." Nettie noticed something on the screen. "Wow, there are a couple people working on your line. I'll have to investigate that."

"Do you think I might have an ancestor in the Civil or Revolutionary War?"

"We'll have to check." Nettie shrugged. "My mother was illegitimate, and I was able to figure out who my grandfather was with DNA. A long-standing mystery solved."

"There's nothing complicated like that in our family," said North with confidence.

Nettie abruptly changed the subject. "What do you think of Miki?"

That question caught North off guard, and Nettie laughed.

"I'm impressed with her. She's always very busy."

"That she is."

"You look tired Mrs. Hol…uh, Nettie."

Nettie leaned her head on the back of her chair. "I'll just rest my eyes, just keep talking. I'm listening. I'm curious what you think of Miki."

"I think it's great that she wants to give the town a shot in the arm, and that she could possibly convince the mayor of her plan. This community always sticks together, so hopefully, he will listen."

North continued scanning the computer, he hadn't looked at Nettie for a few minutes. "I'd like to find a way to stay here forever, even if I don't farm. Do you think Miki would ever want to live here again?"

Nettie didn't respond.

North chuckled when he looked over at Nettie. She was snoring slightly. He looked around until he located a crocheted blanket and covered her. He picked up his keys and quietly let himself out, but before he closed the door, he glanced back at Nettie.

She's definitely listening.

He laughed, locked the door from the inside, and closed the door.

Chapter Eleven

Nettie woke up finding herself alone. She glanced at her clock, *three a.m.*

Her shed had been a Victorian carriage barn when the Doc lived there. Two stories high, it was big enough for two carriages, and a stall for Toby, his chestnut companion, who pulled the carriage for house calls. Upstairs, there was enough room for hay and straw for Toby for a year.

Nettie was glad she had insulated and drywalled the carriage barn and installed the wood burning stove. The heat from the stove blew intense hot air all around her, and she wrapped herself with a fleece blanket. With old friend winter coming, it will be more challenging to keep the old carriage barn cozy.

Nettie walked over to look down on the empty stall and remembered her own dapple grey, Old Glory. But now, there were just a couple bales of straw.

Nettie went down to the stall and sat on one of the straw bales and imagined a small pony, maybe an old companion, that needs adopting. Like her, somewhere to stay to live out its last days. To hear chomping on some oats or pulling hay from the iron hay holder would be so comforting.

Her thoughts took her back to when Noel first had Miki, and they would sit on the bales and beg for a horse. She smiled as she walked back to her desk.

Unexpectedly, her thoughts turned to a baby boy laying in the straw wrapped in a swaddling cloth. She turned around quickly, but there was no baby. She continued walking, her thoughts drifted back many years.

Back at her desk, she picked up a picture of Miki and stared at her granddaughter's beautiful blue eyes and winning smile. Her heart swelled with pride, and her thoughts overtook her.

Her life is so different than mine. I once had beautiful plump skin and thick glossy hair. Things were so different then. No one thought of leaving our hometown, but instead had the same dreams as our parents'; pride in our farms and local stores. Many have been here for generations.

Now that everyone is thinking about the past, maybe I can be useful. Miki is so busy flying on jets to the big city, I wonder if her life will be fulfilling for her. I guess time will tell. It's hard to make a living here now, and the big city offers women endless opportunities. So many choices out there that encourage them to leave our little town.

She returned the photo to her desk and reached an old Roi-Tan cigar box. She opened the lid and pulled out a couple old 4 x 4 black and white photos. One was of two children hugging each other on the church steps, in the background a 1942 Plymouth with a huge hood ornament on the large, rounded hood.

Look at you, Caleb, so young.

She read the names aloud that were on the picture, "Caleb and Antoinette 'Nettie,' about five years old."

The second photo was a grinning Nettie with Caleb kissing her cheek.

Tears trickled down Nettie's cheeks, but then she laid her head on her arm and sobbed. "Caleb, my true friend, I miss you so much."

Finally, Nettie sat up and ran her fingers through her hair. She looked at the picture again. "I've met a new friend, Caleb, his name is North. He wants to learn about his family, and for me, it's like having a grandson. You know how I enjoy family history, and I would love to make him happy."

Chapter Twelve

FRANKLIN GAZED OUT the window as he and Miki wound their way down to Dubuque.

"I love the bluffs here. Look at that tower in the middle of a valley. How did that happen? I suppose it's limestone."

"Yes, I believe so," said Miki.

"It amazes me how the trees dig into the rock and find a home there."

Miki nodded. "That's always amazed me, too." She read the sign to the right of the road. "Dubuque, population 72,481. Off to the big city, well, at least that's what we here in Iowa call a big city."

"You're funny."

"I know, but looks aren't everything."

Franklin laughed. He turned his attention back to the scenery. "Wow, it's amazing, all the limestone cliffs along the river."

"The Mississippi was once much wider."

"Whew, I can't imagine building a bridge over that."

"I guess that would have to be like the Golden Gate Bridge." Miki continued. "Eastern Iowa is the prettiest part of the state."

She pulled into a parking spot and shut the engine off. "When we get inside, I'll do the talking. If you, my fine man, manage the video and pamphlets."

"Got it. When we're finished, let's do some sightseeing."

Franklin opened the back door and grabbed the laptop from of the seat.

They went through the front doors and up a flight of stairs. They could see Joe Holland on the other side of a glass wall.

"Miki!" Joe welcomed them when they stepped through the door. "Good to see you. My, how you have grown, how is your grandmother?

"Oh, she's great, nothing keeps her down."

"No, nothing ever does. She's the most productive senior I know. Other than me, of course." He chuckled and then turned to Franklin.

Miki quickly said, "Mr. Holland, this is Franklin Wimmer, my associate working with Main Street Alive."

Joe extended his hand. "Nice to meet you, Franklin."

Franklin returned the handshake. "You, too, Mr. Holland."

"Please, call me Joe."

"I remember your uncle, Joe, he was like a mascot of our Main Street," said Miki.

"Yeah, our ancestor started manufacturing cutters, or sleighs, right on Main Street. In fact, there are still a few around. I have one in storage, and there are some wonderful restoration companies that make them look brand new. I was surprised to see one for sale in Wisconsin."

"Oh, I would love to ride in it. I've never had that chance. Do you think we could display it in our new museum? Since it's from Elkton," asked Miki.

Joe glanced at his watch. "I'll have to think about that."

"Joe, I know your time is precious. Can we show you thirty seconds of our video? You'll see what Main Street Alive is about, and why I thought of you."

"Sure, I have a few minutes."

Franklin opened his computer and clicked play on the video he had already cued.

Lively music poured from the speaker, and then the announcer's voice. "Main Street Alive! Small towns are America's heartbeat, the hub of our communities, our heritage, and our commerce. How can we preserve the past while staying relevant to all members of the community? Our first step is to preserve our historic building facades. We will cut costs by asking members of our own community to donate their time and skills."

Miki glanced at Franklin, and he pressed the microswitch to stop the video.

Joe is stoic, always so hard to read

"Now, this is what I was thinking for you, Joe. I wondered if you might be interested in purchasing your grandfather's old factory, then restoring the facade to its original look. We are organizing locals to cut some of the cost, mainly woodworking replication. We are thinking your Uncle Woot's would be perfect for that job."

Joe didn't respond right away. After thinking for a few minutes, he said, "I think this is a wonderful idea. I would like to fix up my great-great-grandfather's store, and I know he would have liked that. But, since we moved from the small town, I don't really have any time to spend away from my own business."

"Well, try to imagine how it will be," said Miki. "There's going to be a new subdivision so lots of new families. And Main Street Alive! will draw people from all over the United States. They will come just to see old towns smartly done with a mix of old-world charm and modern conveniences.

"Next door to the former sleigh factory will be a German bakery with a fresh gourmet sandwich shop. The aroma of smoked apple bacon and homemade sarsaparilla will make for a family atmosphere. The ladies have created some new recipes, and Betty's bakery is excited about supplying cinnamon-butter crunch topping on lemony apple pie and cherry-divine popovers. Then, of course, chocolate dipped strawberries in season."

Joe's eyes widened. "Well, that does sound good. Do they still have the Strawberry Festival?"

Miki's voice rose. "Yes! I see you fitting in there like a glove."

"You know now that you bring this up. I do have the original cabinetry and antique desks we pulled out of there when we rented out the property. It's in the back of my factory taking up space that I could use. Maybe we could take some measurements in your museum, see if we have something to help you out. What do you think?"

Miki had a hard time containing her excitement. "I think it's a win-win!" She glanced at Franklin who was grinning.

"Leave me the paperwork, and I'll look over the concept. I'll have to go up there, see what the building needs, and create an estimate. I'm glad you came by young lady. I'll call you back."

Franklin handed him the paperwork, and Joe said, "This is exciting. It would be nice to go up there more often, just to get away."

"Wonderful. My mom and grandmother will be happy to see you around, too."

Franklin shook Joe's hand again. "It was nice to meet you, sir."

"Likewise."

Miki and Franklin all but skipped down the stairs and out the front door.

Once outside, they high fived each other.

Miki was so excited her mind was on fire with more ideas.

Chapter Thirteen

"We must do something fun. How about a funicular."

Franklin looked at her quizzically. "I'm afraid I don't know what that is."

"What? Then let me tell you about it." She laughed. "You will love it.

"It's a system on a very steep railway with two cars, one at the bottom and one at the top. They pass each other as one goes up, and the other goes down. They say ours is the shortest and steepest in the world."

"Okay, I feel like a kid."

Fourth street was a dead-end, and Miki parked at the far end. A small wooden room with glass windows was right in front of them at the bottom of the steep hill. They waited in the little room for the car to come down.

Miki pointed up the hill. "You can see when the two cars pass by each other where the track splits. On the inside, there are three very steep steps on either side for the passengers. The seating matches the incline of the hill."

"Makes me dizzy to look up there. I can't imagine how it feels to be on it."

"Let's find out." Miki pulled the rope attached to a buzzer. "Now the operator at the top of the hill knows we're here."

The greased ropes pulled the car slowly up the rails.

Franklin looked down at the city. "These ropes better hold."

"They usually do."

"What?"

"They have been known to break a few times, and the car shot down the street like a missile."

Miki shuddered. *I better not think about that, I'm scaring myself now.*

The car made it to the top, and Franklin and Miki stepped through the turnstile, paid for the tiny trip, and then walked out to look at the view.

"This is spectacular to see the Mississippi in both directions. Is that the bridge we crossed in the middle of the night?"

Miki nodded. "Uh-huh."

"It's beautiful. What's that old tower?"

"That's the Shot Tower. Built in 1856 if memory serves. It was used to make shot during the Civil War. That's why it's so tall. Molten lead is poured from the top, it falls through different sized heavy screens to create the rounds. In this area, the shot is made from lead, it's a natural resource around here. Europeans discovered the Indians mining it when they first arrived."

"It must have been toxic to them."

"No, surprisingly it's not toxic in its natural state. They melted it into bars and sent it down to St. Louis." Miki shoved her gloved hands up the sleeves of her coat. "It's so cold, I would rather wait till summer to take you down to the river front."

"What about where you grew up?"

"Sure, we can drive by Mom's house."

Back in the car, Miki drove up Dodge Street, made a left on Bryant, and when they reached the top, they were at Mt Loretta.

She pointed to the store on the right side of the street. "In the old days, a horse-drawn trolley used to come up Bryant then turned around right in front of this brick store. It was a grocery store then, owned by a man named Sullivan."

They turned onto Mt Loretta, then drove past a school and an old convent, then turned right on English Lane. About halfway down the hill was an attractive brick home, and Miki pulled into the driveway. She parked the car, then let them in the house with her key.

"I told Mom we would drop by for a sandwich." Miki headed straight for the fridge and opened the door. "Oh, she already made them."

She picked up a note sitting on top of the sandwiches and read, "On the stove is some Fall Sunset herbal tea."

"So, you planned to come here anyway?"

Miki smiled. "Yes, eventually."

"Well, it sure smells good. Where are the cups? I'll pour us some."

They had just finished their sandwiches when Noel came in from the garage. "I'm home!"

"Thanks for the sandwiches, Mom."

"Yes, thanks, they were delicious." Franklin stood. "I should run over to the dry cleaners and pick up my coat."

Miki tossed him the keys to the rental car.

"Be back soon."

Noel said, "I have some art supplies in the attic. My knee is killing me. Could you help me get them down?"

"Sure, I can help you. What will I be looking for?" Miki pulled the ladder from the coat closet and put it beneath the attic hatch. She climbed up a couple steps, removed the cover, and disappeared through the opening. "What am I getting, Mom?"

"Cold pressed paper, the board and paint pallet, and there's a small box of brushes."

"Whew! It's dusty up here," called Miki. She pulled the light switch. Nothing. She leaned down, so her mom could hear her. "The light bulb is burned out."

Noel walked away. "I'll get another one."

The light socket was high above her head, and Miki struggled to align the bulb. She lifted her arms dramatically. "Let there…be light!" She turned the bulb a tiny bit, and it came on. "Ah-ha! I see everything, I'll pass them down to you."

Miki stopped when something caught her eye. "Oh, my gosh, Mom. Here's some of the paintings we did together when I was little. This makes me want to cry."

She looked through the scuttle hole, her mom was standing at the bottom of the ladder. "We have to go through these."

She handed the supplies down to her mother, climbed out of the attic, and placed the cover over the opening.

"Look, Mom, remember this?" She held out a homemade child's book with pages stapled together. "Rain writing. We had so much fun, remember? It rained for days, and I was bored cause I couldn't go out to play, and you told me that you loved the rain, and that I needed a change in attitude. Then you set my little antique school desk over by the sliding glass door and turned on the flood light."

"I remember, the rain started pooling up in the yard," said Noel.

For a few seconds, Miki was lost in the memory of that day.

A bright bolt of lightning lit up the yard, followed by a clap of thunder so loud that it shook the whole house, and it scared Miki. Another bolt of lightning followed and a second clap of thunder, louder than the before. It was right above them, and the windows rattled.

"Perfect for writing," her mom had said, and she had opened the sliding door a little, so they could hear the rain bounce off the tin porch. Then the sky opened, and it poured hard creating a makeshift swimming pool in the backyard. The air was cold and crisp, and they had to put on sweaters to keep warm.

Mom had suggested she work on her book.

"But what will I write about?" Miki had asked, then she decided to write a poem. "But how do I start?'

"Study everything you see and write it down." Mom had said, "We're Rain Writing!"

"We're Rain Writers!" Miki had yelled, and they both had laughed.

"We're a rare breed you know," Mom had said.

Miki was pulled out of her thoughts when her mom mentioned the poem Miki had written that day, and they both laughed reminiscing as they read it.

All of a sudden, Miki felt sad. *For the first time I realize that I never knew what Mom was working on all those years.*

She looked at her mom. "And you were over there working on your book. Where is that book?"

Noel's expression turned sad. "Too many unfortunate things happened."

"What was it about? I have no idea."

"I don't know that you would be interested."

"Of course, I am, Mom. What's the title?"

Mom sighed. "The Edwardian Tourist in My Attic."

"Did you use those two boxes with bundles of letters and old photos?"

"I did." Mom smiled.

It warmed Miki's heart to talk with her mom about this. She said, "Remind me what the letters are about."

"About a man who took a trip around the world in 1909. His name was Albert Perkins, a horticulturist from New York. He was traveling around the world studying horticultural conditions and collecting plants to send to David Fairchild."

"Who's that?"

"He was a brilliant man who was creating the Department of Agriculture. I was going through the divorce at that time. At first, when I got the letters, I wasn't that interested in the history of the world. But then, I started reading them, and I discovered a man who was charming, humorous, and, most of all, newly single. I laughed and cried with his musings and philosophizing. Each country he went to he was fascinated by the common man. The adventures he had and the people he met blew me away. So, I decided to transcribe these letters and really analyze them."

"Who was he writing to?"

"His mother and father in New York, they lived in Newark. They ran a nursery business that specialized in roses. Newark was known as the 'rose capital of America.'"

"Wow, I had no idea."

"Remember? After Dad left, and I bought all those roses and planted them in our yard? They were from Jackson & Perkins."

"So, you were connecting with him. Through his letters."

"Yea, I fell in love with an Edwardian Traveler who died in 1944. Then I started researching every place he went, learning the history of the world as I studied. The internet was becoming easier to use with more content. Remember that old 486 computer?"

"Yeah, Dad bought that for me, my first computer. That thing was huge."

Noel laughed. "I know, they are so different now. Much smaller. Anyway, one day I was searching the New York census of 1870, and I noticed that Albert's father had a middle name of Hinsdale."

"Are you kidding me? We're related?"

"Somehow. I was certain we were. Your grandmother and I searched and searched in Connecticut, but there was one missing link that we could never figure out. So, are we related? I still didn't know. But then, six months ago. I found the missing link."

"Did you finish it, the book?"

"It's lost. The hard drive was defective, and I lost the whole book."

"What?! No, Mom, you need to get started on that book again."

Mom's face lit up. "It's funny, but you're igniting those old feelings I had inside of me. That is exactly what I should do."

"You can get it published. People love stories about traveling to exotic places. But it's time travel, too. I would want to read that book."

"You would?"

"Yes! Wouldn't it feel so good to see your book in a store?"

"Yes, but…"

"But what? What but?"

Noel looked down. "Perhaps I'm too old now, people might think I'm foolish."

"Well, I'm a people. Don't I count?"

"Well, when you put it that way. I guess I've sold myself short."

Miki raised her fist and tried to sound like a New Jersey tough guy. "Ya, what are ya? A man or a mouse?"

They both laughed until they cried.

Noel caught her breath. "Miki, there is so much that I don't know about publishing."

"Mom, do you think I knew how to start a Main Street project?"

"No, I guess you just started without knowing."

"Fuhgeddaboudit." Miki sighed. "Okay, the truth is, I'm so afraid I will fail on the Main Street project and be embarrassed in front of Franklin."

"Really? You always seem so confident, in charge."

"I'm faking it till I make it. Mom, you know what?"

"What?"

"I just realized that I'm competing with him. I secretly want to make it all happen, so I can wow him. I guess I want to impress and make him think I can do anything."

"I think you've already impressed him. I see the way he looks at you."

"Really?"

"I guess we kind of have the same problem, don't we? We both want to be good enough."

Miki asked a little cautiously, "Mom, have you ever seen Dad since the divorce?"

"No. He went to California. I told him to go as far away as possible, and he did. Unless you count Hawaii."

Miki nodded absently. "I expect you to start over on your book, Mom."

They both looked over as Franklin pulled into the driveway.

Mom smiled. "Okay, I will."

"I need to get going, Mom." She hugged Noel, and they both

cried. "I'm so glad I got to help you with this attic project."

"Things couldn't have turned out any better, Miki."

She held her mother at arm's length. "It's no wonder you're so sad, Mom. Taking care of people who have dementia, assisting families with end-of-life issues. You've been doing this for years now."

"It takes a toll, that's for sure. Each time I think I can't do it anymore, then someone needs help. It's hard to find experienced caregivers. I just keep thinking what if it were me?"

"This must be your last job, Mom, it's depressing. You've done a great service to several people, but you are *not* dead, you're an *author*. It's time for you to think of yourself. We're going to start living now…together."

She gave her mom a quick kiss on the cheek, then she turned and walked to the front door, but hesitated and looked back. "Your guardian angel told me in a dream last night that you have only twenty years left, so get going will ya?"

Noel laughed.

Franklin knocked briefly then cracked the front door. "We need to hit the road, Chief."

"I know, I'm coming."

"Thanks for the sandwiches, Mrs. Lewis."

"You're welcome. You kids drive safe."

Noel's heart raced, and she felt like she did on Christmas morning when Miki was little. She looked at Miki's high school graduation photo, lost in the idea of publishing a book.

Chapter Fourteen

IN ELKTON, Granny Keller and a matronly woman in her sixty's spotted a classy woman across the street walking with a tall, handsome man. Assuming the woman was Miki, her anger consumed her. The woman stepped into traffic, dragging Granny Keller with her, ignoring the danger she just put them in.

A man slammed on his brakes to avoid hitting her, and the lady in the car behind him did the same. Drivers rolled down their windows, shaking their fists, and threatening the woman, but she charged forward ignoring all of them.

"Say…" she waved her hand in the air to get Miki's attention. "Hey, my name is Mrs. Krauthammer. Are you the one turning this into a Historic Street?"

"Yes, I'm Miki Lewis. Nice to me…" She reached for the lady's hand, but she was snubbed.

"Well, I don't support it. It will cost too much," the lady snapped.

"But it will bring tourism. You have too many beautiful structures here that will be gone if…"

Mrs. Krauthammer continued. "It's a waste of money. Those buildings have been here over one hundred years. They're not going anywhere."

Miki tried to explain. "I don't think you understand. People travel all over the United States to see Historic Main streets. If it's on a national register, it will bring more young families here, too."

Granny Keller entered the fray. "This is the guy that started this whole mess." Pointing at Franklin, she approached him. "I don't like change. Things are fine the way they are. I'm too tired for all this work. Way to tired."

Apparently, the mayor heard the commotion and ran down the street toward the group.

Franklin tried to settle things down. "Okay, we're not asking for you to do anything, ma'am. We'll find others who are interested in investing."

Embarrassed by the two women, the mayor said, "So much will be done to improve the town."

"Oh, sure, you'll improve it, missy," said Mrs. Krauthammer to Miki. "You'll rack up a big bill and leave town. I wasn't born yesterday!"

"No, that really isn't how this works." Miki protested. "Investors will pay. We'll have younger people volunteering for their community credits."

The mayor guided them away. "Don't worry about Granny Keller, she doesn't even live here. She's from Strawberry Bend."

"Oh," Miki said with relief. "Wait, did you say Keller?"

The mayor waved and ducked into the barbershop.

Miki rolled her eyes as she looked at Franklin. "I'll drop you off at your B&B."

Franklin's phone rang.

"Sounds great. Hang on, Uh-oh, from *Mister* Cousin Dingle, wonder what he wants." He answered the call. "Hi, okay, one sec." He turned to Miki. "I'll walk, I need to talk to him."

Miki kicked off her shoes and flopped on a bed at her grandma's house.

Her phone beeped. She picked it up and tapped the message icon. It was from Franklin.

November 22nd Mr. Dingle is surprisingly happy with my plans for the new subdivision. He wants me back in Chicago (surprise!) and then I'll be traveling home to San Francisco for the holidays. Can't wait to show my family the photos I took. Love your little town.

Miki typed.

Thanks so much for all your help. I've got another Main Street job along Route 66. I start right after the holidays. I'll see you next spring!

She pushed send and plopped back down on her bed.

Chapter Fifteen

THE PROJECT at the museum finally got started. Miki was sweeping the floor, and North was staining some glass display cases.

"I love your Grandma Nettie, she's as sharp as a tack," said North.

"She is, and it's so nice that you can help her, North. I don't like her going up on ladders anymore."

"She does a lot for me, too. She's helping me with my genealogy. I could never afford to pay for that. It's so interesting. I don't know your mother very well. She's only up here on weekends, and I don't want to interrupt her time with your grandma."

"My mom was one of those dragon mothers, always pushing me to achieve. She helped me enter art contests; one year I even won an artist's easel. The best prize ever, though, was a live bunny with a cage. I got to pick out the one I wanted at Kennedy mall. It was a flop eared bunny, mostly white with brown ears and circles around her eyes. I called her Little Anne."

"Like from *Where the Red Fern Grows?*"

"Exactly. I loved that movie. Can you help me carry this rug outside?"

North picked up the other end, and they carried it outside to shake it.

Miki rolled it up, and as she did, she noticed North watching her. She didn't look up.

North's random comment came unexpectedly. "Bunnies are so fun to cuddle, so soft, with cute little noses."

She knew he was flirting with her. She finished rolling the rug and stood up. "Did you have one, too?"

"Huh? Yeah. Yeah, my dad helped me make a cage in the back yard."

They carried the rug back inside.

"So, you're kind of handy?"

"Jack of all trades. I always wanted to be like my dad."

"Did your parents stay together?

"Yes, I have a good mother, too. The best. How about you? Did your parents stay together?"

"My dad was great when I was young. We did so many fun things. But then he started to drink too much when I was in junior high. One night, I needed to get to a play at school, and Dad drove off the road in a ditch. I was so scared. We got there all right. But Mom never trusted him to take me in the car again. So, I guess that's why she's a little jaded. I've seen her crying when she watches a movie that has a good dad in it, then I hear the TV go off. I think she wonders if Dad thinks about us. If he misses us."

Miki finished her breakfast and ran down to the library. She located a phone book.

Most older people still have rotary phones around here.

She flipped the pages until she found the *L*'s in Guttenburg. She searched the list of names.

I know my dad had two sisters in Guttenberg. Thelma and Betty Lewis. That's them!

She closed her eyes for a minute to think how she would approach them.

She dialed the number and listened to it ring on the other end.

"Hello."

"Hi, I'm looking for the sisters of Hank Lewis."

"Yes."

"Is this Aunt Thelma?"

Cautiously, the woman answered, "Yes, but who are you?"

"Well, I don't know you very well…"

Click.

Miki called back.

The phone was answered, but the woman said nothing.

"Please don't hang up! My name is Miki Lewis. My mom is Noel. Hank is my dad."

Sounding relieved, the woman said, "Oh, my…of course, I know who you are. You're my niece, I apologize. There are so many prank callers these days. How are you?"

"I'm fine, ma'am, how are you?"

"Very good. What can I do for you, Miki?"

"I'm looking for my dad. Do you happen to have his phone number? I heard he lives in California…but I don't have any contact information. He does contact me at least twice a year, he sends me money on Christmas and my birthday. Occasionally, he writes a note and says he hopes I'm doing well. But there is never a return address. Could you tell me how he is doing."

Nettie walked by the library. She noticed her granddaughter talking on her cell phone.

Hmm. Wonder what she's up to?

Chapter Sixteen

THANKSGIVING was a beautiful fall day.

Nettie, Noel, and Miki, three generations spent the weekend together cooking their favorite dishes; yams, garlic and cream cheese mashed potatoes, green bean casserole with French onions, and the roasting turkey smell permeated the kitchen. It was enough to make everyone's mouth water.

Miki kept checking her phone to see if she had missed any calls. She checked her messages over and over. Nothing.

Nettie pulled the frosty metal bowl and beaters out of the freezer and put them in front of Noel, so she could make the whipping cream for the pumpkin pie.

"Has there been anything new with my DNA, Mom?"

"No dear, no matches, unfortunately. I check every week."

Miki walked to the front living room window, looked out, and then looked up and down the street. Aunt Thelma had said she would try to get Miki's dad to come on Thanksgiving.

She walked back to the kitchen. Noel was saying, "You don't feel bad about my asking, do you, Mom?"

"Absolutely not. I want you to know about your biological parents. I don't think any of the facts on your Non-Identifying Information are right."

"But you know I love you, don't you?"

"I do dear. I'm just sorry I have not been able to crack this case," said Nettie. "I've never had anything this difficult before."

Miki checked the front window again just as a car pulled up in front of the house. She peered from behind the curtain.

She recognized the two women who got out of the front seats as her aunts Thelma and Betty. Then her dad climbed out of the back seat.

Wow, Dad looks thin.

Miki clasped her hands together.

Oh, please dear God, let this go well.

Miki hurried into the dining room and made room for three more place settings. Then she moved three folding chairs into place, hoping her mom wouldn't notice as she was in a discussion with Grandma.

Noel lined up the serving silver with the appropriate empty dishes in the kitchen.

"You're a whiz at genealogy, Mom. I know you'll find them. It will happen." Noel scoffed.

"I can't help but think your mother might be a pathological liar. She has sure covered her tracks well. I hope when we find her, you won't be disappointed. I also I hope I'm wrong," said Nettie.

Noel sighed. "I just want a chance to see her if she's alive. Does she ever think of me? Did she hold me?"

"I can promise you she did. Who could resist holding their baby," said Nettie sympathetically.

"Maybe, she's looking for me. What if I have siblings? Why did she give me up? What were the circumstances?"

Noel brought the bread and butter to the table.

Miki started to panic. "I'm starting the Christmas music now," she called to whoever was listening. "Perry Como first." She slipped the vinyl record out of its sleeve, then centered the hole on the turntable plate. Her hand shook erratically as she lifted the stylus arm and placed it on the record. Suddenly, she dropped the arm so hard the needle scratched over the first two songs.

Noel rushed into the living room. "Good heavens! What's wrong with you? You're acting like you ate all the pies before dinner. What's going on?"

"Well." Miki waved her arms around nervously and gasped for air. "I have a surprise."

The doorbell rang, and Miki jumped.

Noel stared at her daughter shaking her head as she walked to the front door. Miki followed her mom, who was visibly shocked to see her sisters-in-law standing on the porch.

"Thelma and Betty! This is a surprise. You came all the way out here from Guttenberg?"

"We did," said Betty.

"I haven't seen you for such a long time. Come in, please."

Miki couldn't see her dad, but through the front door, she noticed the neighbors walking their German shepherd. All three stopped and stared at what she could only assume was her dad.

Noel said, "'Would you like to stay for dinner? We can put out a couple more settings."

Noel took a few steps to the entrance of the dining room. She glanced at the table and noticed there were already more settings on the table. Puzzled, she looked over at Miki, and they locked eyes.

Miki looked guilty. She took a deep breath and straightened her shoulders. "A wonderful surprise, isn't it, Mom?"

"Yes, a wonderful surprise." Noel took the ladies' coats and turned her back to them when she reached for a hanger. Then she heard the door open and close.

She turned around and saw only the two women. "Who was that?"

The two aunts acted as though they didn't know what she was talking about.

Then Miki said, "Let me seat you two ladies."

When they walked away, Noel saw Hank with a flower arrangement in his hand, looking sheepish.

Miki's heart pounded in her chest.

The fate of my life rests on this moment.

"Hi, Noel. It's good to see you. You look very nice."

Nettie rushed in and took the table arrangement from Hank. "Oh, this is so lovely, isn't it, Noel?"

"Yes, it's such a surprise, isn't it, Mother?" Nettie prattled to the table with the flowers.

Noel looked Hank up and down. "Where do you live now?"

"Here, in town. I've been sober for ten years now. I know it was my fault that we divorced. I want to apologize to you. Do you think we can be friends? For Miki's sake?"

"Ahhh." Noel looked at her daughter.

"Yes, we can be friends, Hank. I'm proud of you for doing the right thing, and I accept your apology. Would you like to stay for dinner?"

Obviously humbled, Hank pulled his stocking cap off his head. "Could I?" he asked.

Relieved, Miki said, "Let me take your coat, Dad. He looks good, doesn't he, Mom?"

"Miki!" Noel snapped.

"Sorry, Mom."

They walked into the dining room where everyone was smiling.

Miki grabbed his hand and led him to his seat at the end of the table.

Hank stopped. "Oh, I don't know if I should be here." He turned to Noel. "Is this, okay?"

Noel nodded. "Yes, of course."

"Why don't you ask someone to pray, Dad?" said Miki.

The room became tense, and they all looked at each other.

Miki sighed. "Never mind. I'll do it myself."

After the prayer, Hank jumped up. "How about if I carve the turkey and carry it in? It smells delicious. You always were a good cook, Noel." It was obvious he was nervous.

"You were always gracious about my cooking, Hank, and the

flowers were very thoughtful of you. You've always been like that." Noel glanced at Miki. "Remember that beautiful arrangement you got me when Miki was born? The one in the baby carriage. I loved that."

"I didn't really remember what it was," Hank smiled.

"She still has it. Do you want to see it?" Miki started to stand.

"No, Miki. I think you've done enough already," said Noel, and Miki sat back down.

Betty sighed. "When you guys are done reading from Miss Manners, could we have Hank cut the turkey and get it in here! I'm hungry."

Noel laughed. "Betty, you never could hold your feelings. Let's eat."

Everyone relaxed and passed around the dishes overflowing with food. They enjoyed a pleasant dinner together, then Nettie suggested a hand of cards to let dinner settle. "Let's play Euchre," she said.

They cleared the table and divided into two teams. Nettie graciously offered to be on Betty and Thelma's team.

The game got competitive with everyone yelling and throwing cards down in excitement.

After they played two games, the sisters said they were tired and ready to go home.

Noel wrapped some extra pie for them to take home.

Hank dragged his feet to put his coat on.

Noel said, "Hank, I have that third bedroom if you would like to stay for a few days. I can take you home."

"I can take you home, too, Dad," said Miki.

Obviously thrilled with the outcome, Thelma said, "Happy Thanksgiving to all of you, and thank you for the dinner. "

Betty added. "It was delicious, even though it took a long time to get it on the table."

"I'm so glad you came, and you are always welcome," said Noel warmly. "You're always welcome. I haven't played Euchre or laughed so hard since the last time you were here."

Nettie smiled. "It was quite fun."

Hank ran out to help his sisters into the car.

Nettie turned to her granddaughter. "You're full of surprises."

Noel scowled at Miki pretending to be upset, but then they all burst out laughing.

"He looks good, doesn't he?" said Noel.

Miki chuckled when her mom adjusted her top and put on more lipstick.

They all sat around the fireplace eating pie. Miki asked, "Grandma, could you tell us about John Schweikert? What did your ancestors tell you about him?"

Nettie took a deep breath and began. "My three times great-grandfather came here in 1847. There was a migration of Germans looking for farmland. In the old country, only the oldest boy inherited the family farm. Times were very bad in Europe. Mothers watched their children slowly starve to death. Some did the unthinkable and sent them on ships to America, knowing they would never see them again.

"Fortunately, the Germans in America were better off financially, and very organized. When emigrants arrived here, there were organizations to help. They fed them and gave them transportation to a state that was looking for more farmers. John landed in New York, but soon went to Chicago where he found his first wife Wilhelmina. Iowa became a state in 1846, and many farmers came to settle here. You know what? I think next summer we should all go out there and see where the farm is and where the family is buried. Doesn't that sound like a fun trip. I've never seen the property."

"I'll put it on my calendar. I'm not sure when we could fit it in, but I'll try," said Miki. "Franklin and I will be very busy all summer."

Noel asked, "Tell us about when you were a little girl in Elkport, Mom."

"My dad was the last of the farmers in our family. We had a cute little Victorian house. Like all farmers, my mom and dad were hard workers. Dad's brother died when a tractor rolled over on him. That whole community came to his funeral. Farmers' relatives from as far away as Dubuque came and milked for them. The pain we felt as a community, it was devastating. People had respect for each other. Everyone knew that 'but for the grace of God, it could be any of them next.' They loved their farms, and the day after the funeral, they got up and carried on. Salt of the earth people."

"Tell us about your beau." Miki beamed.

"Caleb?"

"Yes, why didn't you marry him? What was he like? Was he handsome?'

"Oh, yes, he was handsome. Dark brown hair and blue eyes and… very kissable lips!" They all laughed like they were at a slumber party.

Nettie continued. "His dad worked at the bank down there and had a farm. Peter was Caleb's father. They had a little farm with hogs and chickens. Caleb sold eggs. He always had an artist's temperament, though."

"Sounds like you guys were a lot alike," said Hank.

"Yes, I guess we were.

"When there was time, we loved to play at the Turkey River. We'd try to catch little guppies and water skaters that glided on the top of the water. It was impossible, of course, but it didn't stop us from trying. How many sunny carefree days we spent by the river. We had jars of grasshoppers and lightening bugs and pockets of marbles. Hard to believe, but they were a big deal back then. Somebody had the rim of a bicycle wheel, and we'd chase that down the road with a stick. We would play with my dog Tammy, and sometimes we would ride my horse, Old Glory. We were always scheming and laughing. We were just two peas in a pod. I have pictures in my Roi-Tan box."

Noel asked, "Could you turn over the record, Miki. Does anybody else want a cup of hot chocolate?"

"Yes. Sounds perfect," said Hank.

Nettie pulled the Roi-tan box from her purse and opened it. She lifted a picture. "Here's one of us in front of the church."

They all took turns looking at the picture.

"One more story, Grandma, about Old Glory this time," said Miki.

Nettie smiled, and her eyes sparkled. "Yes, that was my horse. A dapple grey, a real beauty; we were inseparable. I always wanted a horse, you know, girls and horses." Nettie sighed. "You would have all loved Glory. I adopted her."

Noel said, "What? You never told me any of this."

Miki took a sip of her chocolate. "This is so much fun."

"Well, people really couldn't afford horses back then. It was still the depression for us, and they were just an extra expense. One day, Papa was making a delivery to a farm, and he invited me to go. No one answered the door. So, we went to the barn where there was a lot of consternation. There on the floor was a dapple-grey, she was struggling for air, and the vet was bent over her.

"The vet stood and said, 'All you can do is put her down. There's nothing else I can do. Do you want me…'

"The horse's owner said, 'No, I can't afford it.'

"Papa and I watched the vet leave. The farmer lifted his gun from the rack on the wall. It was awful to hear the shot hit its mark."

"It startled me, and when I flinched, something in the dark also flinched, but it fell back into shadows. I tried to see what it was through my tears. I stared into the darkness until a curious figure moved toward me into the light. It was a tiny four-legged filly. The mare on the ground had just given birth! I was sad for them both. She couldn't nurse from her mama now, and she seemed to sense her life was in danger.

"The farmer looked at the filly and said sadly, 'She's not going to make it.'

"She could barely stand on her spindly, shaking legs, and I begged my father to let us take her home. My dad spoke to the farmer and offered to take the filly off his hands, to let me work with her.

"'My daughter really wants a horse, but I can't afford to pay any-thing,' my dad told him.

"He readily consented. 'I'm done with horses. They cost too much and serve no purpose anymore.'

"We took her home in the cab of our old truck, and I held her in my lap. She was so cute with her tiny soft nose and long eyelashes around her big liquid eyes. I got some milk from the cow and added corn sugar and fed her bottles of it every day. I threw a blanket over the straw in a stall, then I put my arm around her warm neck. How could I not adore her? To my delight, she lived and thrived.

"At four o'clock the next morning, Papa came to check on us before milking. He said I needed to get my chores done, that the filly was extra work.

"Then he smiled and said to me, 'Antoinette, adoption is a way to pass love around. Think how happy her mama is in heaven.'

"The newborn put on a show jumping and running with her rubbery tendons. Then she nudged me and snuggled up to me.

"My dad said, 'You adopted that little filly, and all she wants is you now. I'm proud of you. It's like my great-grandfather leaving Germany to come to America. America adopted our family, and now you are here to enjoy it. That's why I always fly Old Glory over the door. I always want to remember God's blessings to our family.' Then he asked me what I was going to call her?

"I remember standing in the doorway staring at the American flag. I told my dad I would call her Old Glory. He liked the name. My dad put a pipe in his mouth, patted Old Glory's head, and left the barn. I stayed there running the back of my fingers along Glory's white blaze, then I told her, she would always be mine. She seemed to understand, and I nestled her furry head under my jaw, and then she licked my cheek."

Chapter Seventeen

THE DAY AFTER Thanksgiving, Noel and Hank sat on a bench at Cleveland Park overlooking the Mississippi River and the Julien Dubuque Bridge. They held hands like high schoolers again. They talked about their memories of growing up in Dubuque.

Noels teeth started to chatter. "You know what? This is what I've really missed."

"Your teeth chattering?"

"No goofy. I felt so sad about not having a history with someone who cares about me. It's so important."

Hank wrapped his arms around her, and they walked back to the car.

Chapter Eighteen

THE NEXT DAY, Miki drove Nettie back to her house in Elkton. Miki worked by day, and in the evenings, she helped Nettie get all her Christmas houses up. One at a time, the older woman carefully placed each house and figurine into a specific spot paying attention to detail. You would have thought people really lived in the houses the way Grandma treated them. She sculpted snowbanks for the Victorian sledders to play on, placed a tiny snowman nearby, and a scrubby tree chewed by her dog when she was a puppy.

Nettie looked at her little dog. "Gingersnap, where's your coat? You'll get cold. Oh, I forgot, it's in the dryer." The dog's sweater was green and red with a gingerbread man on the back, and Nettie pulled it on Gingersnap.

"Your mommy loves you, Miss Ginger," said Nettie, and Miki laughed.

"It's so nice to spend time alone with you, Grandma. I've been away for so many years. And I know we will still have many Christmases to come, but somehow this year feels very special to me. I feel like my life will take another turn. I'm thinking about what it would be like to have children and wondering where I would live."

"Really? I'm so happy."

"I'd like to have several, so I don't want to wait too long."

"Is there someone special you have in mind?"

"Not yet. But being back here made me realize that I would like to raise a family here. I loved my childhood."

"Me, too. Don't you just love Bing for Christmas?"

Miki stood and laughed again. "Yes, and I will go put on a record."

"I'm dreaming of a White Christmas," Nettie sang softly.

Miki looked out the window of the front door. "It's snowing. Very dry and crystal like." She sang with her grandma, "Just like the ones I used to know."

They laughed together and opened the living room shades. They curled up on the coach in blankets and watched the first snow fall under the streetlights.

"I love you, Grandma."

"I love you, too, Granddaughter."

Chapter Nineteen

ON New Year's Eve, Nettie nestled up to her laptop with a cup of hot apple cider and caramel creamer. She opened the laptop and plugged in the power cord.

My sessions are always too long for the life of the battery.

On Family Core Genealogy site, a search of Karl born in 1918 connected her back yet again to his father Karl C. She read out loud, "In the 1880 census as blacksmith in Elkport."

As the hours passed, she found the Keller family reached back to the Civil War where an ancestor served the Union Army at the Battle of Pea Ridge in Arkansas. "The Iowans served there to keep Missouri from becoming a slave state. It also opened the door to keeping Arkansas a free state. Wow, that's something to be proud of."

The next week, North came to snow blow Nettie's driveway and sidewalk and put salt on the cement. North invited himself into the shed.

"I pressed on till five in the morning last night," said Nettie.

North sat on the couch next to her. "Pea Ridge was a funny name."

"I know, I had to look it up to remind myself what the story was. I had an ancestor in another battle down there. They said the name came from a narrow row of houses, on the side of a mountain in the Ozarks. The Native Americans planted hog peanuts or turkey peas there before the Europeans arrived, and the name stuck. There's a map of the battle, but I'm going to let you explore that. I'm going to hit the high points. Do you want to hear another story?"

"Yes."

"Your mother's maternal line has a real surprise. Do you recognize this?" She held up some pictures she copied from the internet.

North studied the photo of a car. "A Studebaker? I've heard of them. They stopped making those a long time ago."

"How about this man? Do you recognize him?"

"He has a lot of hair; I hope that happens to me, and quite a beard. What's his name?"

"John Mohler Studebaker. John and his brother founded Studebaker back in 1852 in South Bend, Indiana. Look at this." She held up a picture of a beer wagon pulled by eight famous horses.

"Oh, those are Clydesdales."

"Yes. Your ancestor made that wagon before he started making cars. I read that they started as blacksmiths, then they began making horse-drawn wagons, and when the Civil War broke out, their biggest customer was…"

"The government? So, he was making wagons for a war my other ancestor was in? That's a weird thought."

"I'm telling you, the more I do genealogy, the more I find the world is a very small place. We are all interconnected in some way. People think because there are so many of us, it doesn't matter anymore how we treat each other. I don't believe that."

She held up another picture of John Studebaker. "I'd like to introduce you to your four times great-grandfather."

North studied the picture closely. "I have his blood running through my veins. And my great-grandfather was also a blacksmith." He stared at it a longtime contemplating. "It must have been a lowly job."

"No, blacksmiths were very valuable to the community and were part of the more well-to-do people in town. They were highly skilled."

"I can't wait to do more research into all these topics. I wonder if his shop has become a historic landmark."

"It's a National Museum."

"I would love to see South Bend now. Way better than Strawberry Bend. They probably have a streetlight there. Maybe Dad would go there with me."

After North left, Nettie headed to the fridge for an ice pack for her aching arm.

Downloading twenty-five hundred documents to a tree will do that to you.

She stumbled to the bedroom and collapsed on the bed.

It was so much fun to wow North. I wonder how many more surprises there will be.

Nettie laid in the dark then realized she left Gingersnap alone, and now she was whimpering at the side of the bed.

"Okay, little friend, come to Mommy."

Chapter Twenty

NOEL AND HER MOTHER'S COMMITTEE had been busy painting the rooms in the museum a light mint green to contrast with the wide oak wood trim. Now they were ready to create wall displays. In one room, mounted quilt samples were hung on the wall to inspire the children.

Nettie asked Miki to take notes, while she spoke to the committee. "We'll need glue and construction paper, so the kids can create a design for a quilt. Another room has mounted photos of the founding fathers of the town along with photos of their businesses. I think this should be a lifestyle room, too. How they lived, their transportation, and the clothing they wore."

Nettie brought out four letters and announced to the committee, "Four schools have committed to coming next year to our new program, and there's more. An anthropology student from the university will come and build a miniature bark lodge for the Native American room and bring arrowheads and other artifacts. The Ranger Park Service has offered to donate roadkill pelts of several different animals."

Chapter Twenty-One

NETTIE STRETCHED her neck from side to side, opened search on her computer browser, and added another Keller name. She soon found an ancestor in Pennsylvania, and a cemetery that held all the first pioneers of that state. She found pictures on a family tree posted by another branch of the family.

Wow, North will love this.

After downloading five thousand and twenty-three documents and filling eighteen pedigree charts, she hit a dead end.

"Well, Ginger, should I see what I can find?"

Gingersnap barked.

"Okay, I'll get you a treat first."

Nettie sat back down to study the screen. She blinked and rubbed her eyes.

I sure wish I knew what happened to my computer glasses.

Gingersnap barked at her again.

"Okay, I'll give you a chew stick."

Nettie bent over and tried to stick the treat in the corner of the dog's bed.

"What is going on here?" She reached into the corner of the bed and pulled out a washcloth, underneath she found her glasses.

"You sweet thing. You love me so much you wanted my glasses?"

Nettie thought Ginger looked guilty, and the dog wagged her tail.

"Guilty as charged, ay?"

Back to work. Let's look at this female line and see where it goes.

Hours passed. Nettie compared it to peeling an onion. Suddenly, she read out loud, "North had an ancestor in Massachusetts who was in the Revolutionary War!"

She located the military record and read again. "He was part of the Lexington Alarm and was a Minute Man who answered Paul Revere's call to protect Lexington and Concord."

This proves out my theory. We're all connected in some way. You simply must look long enough.

She patted Gingersnap's head. "You know, I have a female line that was in the Lexington Alarm. I wonder if they knew each other."

Nettie yawned and said, "It's four am, time to hit the sack my little Sand Man."

The wiener dog started jumping up and down and followed her into the bedroom.

Chapter Twenty-Two

IT WAS MAY, and spring filled the air. Miki bustled about town talking to carpenters and project leaders. Two boys had volunteered to help with deliveries. AJ would deliver the gingerbread for the storefronts, and Jimmy would deliver the hardware.

Miki said, "We need to check the labels and send these pieces out to each address on Main. This one is 345." Miki wrote the number on a box then on the next one. "And this one is 370," she said as she wrote on the box.

"What's the difference. They all look the same," asked AJ.

"Oh no, they have different angles. See the point at the top of this building? These brackets must fit exactly. The pitch of this roof is much steeper that the one across the street. See what I mean?" Miki pointed to the roof lines.

"Yeah, now I do. I've got it, Miki."

"Make sure they go to the team manager."

"Okay." AJ took the box and walked out the door.

Miki felt like she was in her element, but something was missing. Or not missing. Franklin drove up in a rental. As soon as she saw him, she dropped everything and walked down the street to greet him. They were both grinning from ear to ear.

Franklin climbed out of the car and gave her a hug. "How are you?"

"Good."

"You look good." Franklin smiled.

"Thanks." Miki smiled back.

Jimmy said, "Miki, I need your help."

"You've got the hardware. We need these delivered to each restoration site. I'll put the address right on the box. See your friend up there. Just follow him. The numbers are on the box."

Joe Holland waved as he approached Miki and Franklin. "Miki! I've been looking for you."

Joe said, "I got so excited about the project. I found a guy who restores sleighs. You must see it."

The three jogged down the street.

Joe had driven a small truck to bring the sleigh, and it was being unloaded. Some residents of Elkton gathered around.

Miki drooled. "What a beautiful sleigh. It looks like a sports car with all the fancy trim work, and I love the red color. The design is so Victorian."

"The cushioned seats are authentic horsehair," said Joe.

"The brass trim is so beautiful. It's a dream," said Miki.

Miki heard sleigh bells. She turned around and saw a man leading a horse.

"This my brother, Dale, you want to go for a ride, don't you?" asked Joe.

"This is all your fault, you know. Now I'm hooked." Miki laughed.

Joe pointed to a flatbed trailer. "You can use it in parades all year long if you want."

"Wow, you thought of everything," said Franklin.

"Isn't it wonderful." Miki squealed, and the three men laughed.

Dale's brother brought over a small Belgian horse, brown with a creamy colored mane and tail. The beautiful horse was practically gleaming and perfectly brushed with gold glitter on his hooves. Radiant silver bells over rich conditioned leather literally shined.

Joe explained. "We bought the old factory, and now a magazine wants to interview us about its history. We're doing a photo-op with the first sleigh. Come get in the picture, Miki, you, too, Franklin."

They all climbed in the sleigh, and the horse pulled them down Main Street. As they passed, workers stopped to take in the beauty of it. Miki, Franklin, and Joe waved as though in a parade, and all the people clapped for them. When they caught up to Nettie, she climbed on board.

"This is so thrilling," said Nettie. "I feel like a girl." Tears ran down her face, and everyone cheered.

The sound of the rhythmic clopping of hooves on the pavement and the bells jingling created an atmosphere of nostalgia. They rode up and down the streets as everyone ran out of their houses to see the cheerful commotion and take a picture. Photographers were able to get several great photos.

Joe said, "I've decided to turn the first floor of my great-great-grandfather's store into a sleigh museum. It will tell all about the manufacturing aspect, and in time, I'll have three sleighs. The sleigh restoration company is on the hunt for any Holland cutter they can find."

The horse took a turn left and then left again passed Nettie's house.

"Oh, and the desks I don't need are for the museum. They should have already been delivered."

"Thank you, Joe, we need them," said Nettie.

Neighbors ran outside to see where the bell sounds were coming from, and children squealed with delight as they ran after the sleigh.

"It's great to see all the work being done on the facades," said Joe. "I can't wait to see the finished products."

"We'll put lighted banners over the street in different places," said Miki.

Nettie grabbed Joe's arm. "Thanks, Joe. This made me feel young again. This sleigh would be great for the Grand Marshall of the Christmas parade. Don't you think, Miki?"

"Your right, Grandma, it would."

Chapter Twenty-Three

IT WAS EARLY when North showed up at Nettie's place. He uncovered the roses on the front edge of her property. Then began to hoe a row along the hedges around the front of her house. He had noticed a storm moving in on his drive over.

I'm planting just in time. The seeds will get a good soak. Zinnias and Nasturtiums will be nice and showy from the street.

Nettie came out on the porch. "Good morning, North. Thanks for doing all of this. What are you planting?"

"Some of you favorites, I hope."

She looked at the seed packs. "I do love these. They will be beautiful."

"You won't believe what I found last night, North. When it starts to rain, come inside, and I'll show you." She looked up at the darkening clouds. "Such a shame it had to rain today. They're getting so much done up on Main."

The workers and volunteers on Main started packing up their tools to get out of the coming storm.

Miki walked down to the museum as the rain began to fall. Soon, big fat drops hit her face and arms, and she opened her umbrella.

Once all the equipment was loaded, everyone escaped into their vehicles and left.

Miki had an appointment with the anthropologist who was coming to look at the space he had been allotted, and she met him in the museum.

"It's this corner right here. It's about six feet by eighteen. We can make it tall enough to walk in if you like."

Miki showed him a rough sketch of the plans. "I hope that fits in the budget."

"I'm going to volunteer. But the materials aren't free except the bark. Maybe we could get some real tree branches and put them in buckets with rocks. We should have an iron kettle or even a plastic one would be okay. Maybe we could make a display of how the Indians caught fish in a stream. And of course, a fire pit, and maybe a campfire and some animal skins."

"Do you think four hundred dollars would do it? We could add more later, if necessary."

"I think so, if we need to start with less, it's okay."

"All right, just get back with me. Thank you for coming today. Please take my card if I can answer any questions, just call me."

After the rain started, North studied the pedigree chart on the new family tree additions at Nettie's.

"Look at this, the Civil War, the Revolutionary War? I can't believe how far this goes back. The Massachusetts Bay Company? I remember everyone at school talking about their ancestors' story in junior high, but I had no idea my ancestors played a part. It would have made it so much more meaningful if I had known."

Nettie added. "I have an ancestor in the Massachusetts Bay Colony, too. Our ancestors must have known each other. They helped found towns south of Boston and then went on to Connecticut to start more towns. Maybe somehow, we're related. I've checked but haven't found anything yet."

"I don't know how to pay you back, Nettie. I'm so grateful. It's like God knew I needed you, and he put us together."

"I feel something special about you, too, North. It has been so special to work on this with you."

"Analyzing these pedigree charts has given me so much to think about my ancestors, and everything they did in their lives. It has changed how I feel about myself. To think of my ancestors founding new towns, and that they may have met George Washington, the greatest man who ever lived according to King George III. I can't wait to tell my dad."

North's emotions overcame him, and he pulled Nettie into a tight hug. His feelings for his ancestors combined with his love for Nettie had formed a powerful unexpected bond between him and his new grandma figure.

He would treasure her forever.

Chapter Twenty-Four

THE WHOLE TOWN was alive with excitement while setting up stations for construction on Main Street. The rain had finally stopped, and the youth group assembled saws in one of the buildings.

The youth were cutting with the teacher's assistance, while others worked at the sanding table. The measurements for the boards to be fluted and needed more expertise had been taken care of earlier by Uncle Woot. Once a piece was completed, it was passed down to the older boys to be sanded.

The window company arrived with the new double pane, energy efficient windows while the old ones were being removed. Large blue metal waste containers were left on the street. Some teenage boys had fun carrying the old windows and heaving them into the trash, every young boy's dream.

Scaffolding was set up for the painters now that construction was nearly completed on the six buildings targeted for restoration.

The mayor enlisted the help of 4-H girls to paint the trim boards.

Locals who drove by couldn't help but feel the wonderful energy surrounding the projects. A passerby asked if he could help and soon returned with his own sander and scrapers.

Miki, Nettie, and Noel, and the ladies' committee had gathered at the museum to clean and repair the walls. Four older men had been working on the built-in shelves. They had to pull them out, repair them with glue and nails, and then wash them with wood soap. Once they had thoroughly dried, they applied tung oil to bring out the grain and make them look new again.

Some of the farm ladies provided water and homemade chocolate chip cookies, and the cheerleaders from the high school worked on cleaning the glass on the newly reconstructed display cases.

Miki stepped through the front door of the museum when a truck pulled up carrying four beautiful maple trees. Right behind the truck, Jack Hayes parked his pickup truck and called to Miki. "I have a mini excavator, could you use some help planting those trees?"

Miki was blown away by all they were accomplishing working together.

"You are an answer to my prayers," she told Jack, and she showed him the plans for the trees' locations. He made a phone call, and within minutes, his two sons arrived and pitched in to help their dad.

The mayor and town council showed up with root beer and pizza for lunch, and Miki marveled at everyone's huge appetites as they sat around together eating and joking.

This would never happen in the city; this is Team Elkton.

Chapter Twenty-Five

NETTIE GLANCED at her wall calendar. Today's date was emphatically circled in red.

She picked up the receiver of her old desk phone and began to dial the number. The phone's rotary dial spun back into place every time she released it.

Someone answered, and Nettie said, "Hello, Fern? This is Nettie. Is my special order ready yet?"

"Yes," Fern's scratchy voice answered.

Nettie hurried and got dressed and then drove to the bakery. She paid for her order and excitedly walked back to her car.

Miki drove by the bakery just as her grandma closed her car door. *Hmm, wonder what's that all about, she does this every year.*

She drove around the block and then into a parking lot and headed into the bakery.

Miki greeted Fern. "Hi! Did my grandmother pick up her special order? What was it again? I can't remember?"

"Yes, and it was a mini cake."

"Okay, thanks." Miki waved and walked back out the door.

Nettie heard a car pull into her driveway. She peeked through the curtain. It was Noel.

Nettie remembered the pink cake box and quickly hid it under the counter.

Noel came through the front door, just as her mom slipped the box out of sight. "Hi, Mom."

Nettie tried to act nonchalant. "How was your day, young lady?"

"Mom, I'm not young anymore. If you looked at me occasionally, you might know that." Noel sighed. "How was your day? I mean the part when you're not sneaking around."

Nettie's eyebrows narrowed. "What's that supposed to mean?"

Noel didn't answer.

"The truth?" said Nettie.

"No, tell me a lie," Noel said flatly.

"That's not funny. It's mean," said Nettie.

"It was an emotional day. I have two clients, and one died this morning. I promised her I would be there when she died, and I let her down. She has no family or a single person to care. She's the one with multiple sclerosis, and I've been taking care of her for almost ten years. She was my friend."

"She knew you loved her, Noel. Sometimes, we over promise. We mean well, but we're not superman. She was probably thinking about you because you've been her friend so long, you gave her the gift of love."

Noel sighed. "I'm sorry I lashed out at you. You didn't deserve that. I'm realizing I'll be forty-six this year, and how old is my biological family? They're starting to get up there, and I'm afraid that they will die before I ever meet them. I don't think about it all the time, but having my client die made me project it onto my parents. I made myself crazy with it"

She picked up her spare shoes and a tote bag and walked to the front door.

Nettie followed her. "Drive safe, dear. I don't believe your friend would want you to punish yourself. She can see the bigger picture now. We're the ones with the disadvantage."

Noel gave her mom a quick hug. "That's a very wise thought, Mom. I'll go with that."

Nettie stood on the porch until Noel drove away. She picked a couple of flowers by the front stoop and went back inside.

Nettie heard another car out front, but she retrieved the cake and set it next to her purse on the dining room table.

The door opened, and Miki walked in. "I saw you at the bakery just now, Grandma."

Nettie answered from the next room, "Really?" She came into the dining room. "It's just a little gift for a sick friend."

"That's nice of you," said Miki.

"How's the project going?"

"Joe's contributions really helped. He said the magazine article will be coming out in the December issue."

Nettie walked over to the sink. "That's exciting." She filled a vase with water for the flowers.

"He made our day didn't he. I always liked his family, especially, Uncle Woot. He made the gingerbread for the facades, and now he's working on a sign for the museum. But there's still the old bank block that doesn't have a buyer. In fact, the whole building is for sale. So distressing."

"Oh, that's nice," said Nettie absently.

"Not really, Grandma." She picked up the receipt for the cake, then immediately dropped it on the counter when Nettie turned around. "I better take off. I have pick up some fabric for the costumes."

"Okay, no problem, see you later."

Miki started her car. *Grandma is a little distracted.*

She thought about what she had seen under "directions" on the receipt.

"I love you, Emmanuel." Hmmm.

She stared down the street.

<h1 style="text-align:center">Chapter Twenty-Six</h1>

At the museum, Suzie Jones, Miki, and old Mrs. Krauthammer came over with sewing machines. Miki spread the fabric out on long tables and set up the ironing board.

Miki looked around at the volunteers. "Navy and Jemma, do you think you could help me?"

"Will we get to wear these?" asked Navy.

"Yes. When the children go on a tour of the museum, they get a class picture taken, but I'll let you girls put them on, and I'll take your picture," said Miki.

"Let's lay out all the different fabric and see which pattern will fit each one."

"I can iron," said Suzie.

"Okay." Miki glanced out the window. *There's Grandma.* She turned to Suzie. "Can I borrow your car for a little bit?

"Sure." Suzie tossed her the keys.

"I'll be right back. I'll pick up the fabric, too." Miki grabbed a big hat and a scarf on the way out the back door. She jumped in Suzie's car and headed in the direction Nettie was going.

Staying just far enough behind Nettie's car, she drove around the bend and onto a county road that meandered all around the edge of Turkey River. Trying to stay inconspicuous, Miki almost lost her several times.

After about twenty minutes, Nettie turned left and up into a small family cemetery between two farms. She wound around the narrow roads and finally parked. Miki turned in and parked. She casually walked toward Nettie, staying out of sight, sometimes ducking behind some lilac bushes.

Her grandma was sitting on a lawn chair in front of a large upright stone, softly crying. She opened the cake, stuck a candle in the middle, and lit it.

Miki could hear her softly singing.

Nettie blew out the candle, and then ate a piece of cake. She put a piece on top of the headstone and watched when a few birds flew close, then landed, and pecked at the cake.

Miki quietly turned, retreated to her car, and drove back to Elkton.

Chapter Twenty-Seven

THE PATTERNS were all laid out when Miki got back to the museum with the fabric. She matched the donated ribbon with each costume. "We'll have to buy some more eyelet lace, probably more fabric, too."

Suzie picked up a bolt of fabric. "I love working with gingham and quilting fabric. The children are going to love these dresses."

"Someone also donated some nice pieces of velveteen," said Miki. "We're going to use the costumes for a class picture at the end of the day."

Grandma Nettie walked in. She looked at her granddaughter. "What can I do to help?"

Miki smiled. "Do you want to start cutting the fabric, Grandma?"

"Sure."

Suzie stood. "I need to get the girls home for swimming lessons. I can come back later in the week, though."

"Okay, thanks for your help today, Suzie." Miki turned to Nettie. "Well, I guess it's you and me, Grandma. Let's see how many of these we can get cut out."

"I'll start right here with you, it's easier to visit. Do you like working with Franklin?"

"Yeah, he's a nice guy. He wants me to call him Lin now."

"Oh, that's a new development." Nettie chuckled.

"At first, I thought he was so annoying, but I've really come to appreciate him. We work well together; we just get each other. Well, when he's not annoying me."

"He's very handsome."

"Yeah, he is." Miki grinned.

"Do you think there could be something more?"

"I think he likes me. I'm not sure…but I think he wanted to kiss me once." Miki's eyes narrowed, but then she laughed.

"You know who I really like? This will sound weird I suppose."

"Well, tell me. I'm in suspense."

Miki stopped what she was doing and looked at her grandma. "North."

"North? I do like him."

"We spent the afternoon together yesterday."

"Really? Doing what?"

"We were talking about Elkton. He really loves this place. He appreciates that I'm working so hard to improve it," said Miki. "On the other hand, Lin has enjoyed laying out the new subdivision, and he's good at it, but what connection does he have to this place? He's a big city boy. I'm not sure how he feels about living in a place like this."

"Did you ask him?"

"No. Not exactly."

"So, what did you do with North?"

"Well, he mentioned that there was a whole room full of blacksmithing tools, equipment, and a furnace to boot. We talked about it in depth; how we could use it at the museum. What the lesson would be about."

"Is the blacksmithing set up at Strawberry Bend?" asked Nettie.

"No. Down at Elkport, that ghost town. He says the Keller family used to have a blacksmith shop down there. He checked with his granny. She told him that the blacksmith shop is still standing. It's one of the buildings to be razed, and she has the key to it. So, tomorrow, we're going up there to meet North's family and Granny to try out the key."

"Good idea. Wouldn't it be great to have a blacksmith shop downstairs at the museum? We could do demonstrations."

"That's what I was thinking. The kids would love that."

Miki's phone beeped. "Message from Lin, he's here. He'll be right over."

Chapter Twenty-Eight

FRANKLIN PULLED his car up on the gravel driveway at the back of the building. Miki ran downstairs and outside. Her heart skipped a beat when she saw him, and she ran to hug him. He hugged her back, and then he held her face in his hands. "You've gotten prettier while I was gone!"

Miki laughed and pulled on his hand. "C'mon, Grandma's upstairs."

Franklin followed her. "Lead the way. I haven't been here before."

"The sheriff called a while ago and said we have permission to go down to Elkport," said Nettie.

"That place has been haunting me since I first saw it. Every time I turn around, it pops up in conversation," said Franklin.

"I can't believe you said that. When we were in Chicago, I dozed off in the chopper, and I dreamed about a church with a very large moon behind it. Very odd. I have no idea why. I dreamed I was walking up narrow stairs to a belfry. Then I saw these boys flying up in the air as they pulled the bell. And I looked out the belfry, and something upset me. I was holding my hands over my ears; the bells were so loud. And something flew by. I can't describe it. It flew. The more I think of it, the more I remember."

"It's a mystery," said Franklin as they reached the top of the stairs.

"Nice to see you, Franklin," said Nettie. "Glad you're here. North called, we're meeting him at ten in the morning and heading to meet his family in Strawberry Bend. North has been over at Elkport doing an archeological dig of sorts. He said he's finding some things for the museum."

Miki's eyes sparkled. "I can't wait to see what he found."

Chapter Twenty-Nine

MIKI BACKED her car out of Nettie's garage, and North, Franklin, and Nettie climbed in for the half hour trip to the Keller's house. At the crest of a hill and rounding the curve, Strawberry Bend came into view. The quaint little village unfolded before them with one main street and a handful of side roads.

Franklin pulled a face. "How did I know there would be a giant strawberry involved? That's a huge berrybaloosa on top of a tiny city hall. That's what I call *local* representation. How big is that thing?"

"Fifteen feet high and seven feet wide to be exact," said Nettie.

Franklin looked at her in amazement. "I can't believe you knew that. Stop here, I want to get a picture."

"I'll take it for you," said Nettie.

"C'mon, North, it's your hometown."

North ran over to put his arm on Franklin's shoulder. Nettie suggested Miki stand between the two men before she snapped the photo, and they side-glanced each other.

Several old trucks and station wagons, all badly in need of a good washing, drove down the street. Some had messages scrawled in the dirt.

WASH ME!

HOW MUCH WILL YOU PAY ME TO WASH YOU?

Followed by, NOTHING — GET YOUR CHORES DONE

"Why don't they ever wash a car around here?" asked Franklin. "Their favorite past time seems to be writing on their dirty cars."

"Good question," said Miki.

"This place is so small there aren't any streetlights," said Franklin. "Unreal."

Miki turned down the dirt road, and the car was immediately engulfed in a thick cloud of dust. Franklin started coughing. "Do you have the air on, Miki? I can't breathe."

Miki pulled up to the Keller driveway, turned off the engine, and climbed out. She had put on her work overalls today. "Well, I did warn you." She wrote on her own car, *Miki was here!*

North joined in and wrote, *Nettie has legs like spaghetti.*

Nettie drew a heart and put Miki and a plus sign and a question mark inside.

On the other side of the car, Lin drew a heart, *Lin + Miki.*

Laughing, the three walked to the farmhouse.

"What a beautiful stone house. I love all the flowers." Miki was completely enthralled. "Zinnias of every color, and they must be two feet high." She admired their lush red, yellow, and orange blooms.

Nettie stayed behind to gather up some pedigree charts. She walked by the hearts on the car and took a double take at one, *Lin + Miki.* She rubbed it out with her sleeve and hurried to catch up with the others.

A couple of ducks were swimming in little pond to the right of the house, behind it were rows of recently stripped concord grape vines. A black lab stretched out on the grass and didn't even flinch when one of the duck's walked over and sat on the dog's head.

Startled, Franklin said, "Did you see that? A duck sat on the dog's head."

Beatrice Keller welcomed them wearing a full lacy apron with large pockets on the front. She picked up the bottom of her apron, drying her hands. "They're always like that, you'll always find them together won't find one without the other. They're best friends."

Just then the duck jumped off and walked away, and the dog slowly stood and followed.

"C'mon," said Beatrice, "we can talk while I work. I'll see if I can gitcha the information you need."

North touched his grandmother's arm. "Grandma, I want to introduce you to my friend Nettie. She's the one who found you're descended from the Studebaker family."

"Hi, Beatrice, nice to meet you." Nettie reached out to shake hands.

Beatrice ignored the gesture and said matter-of-factly, "I don't understand people who want to root around in other people's family business."

North was caught off guard by her response and wasn't surprised when Nettie left and joined Franklin.

Franklin stayed outside still intrigued with the animals. "That's the darndest thing I've ever seen." He took some more pictures.

They followed Beatrice into the backyard where sour red cherries weighed down the heavily ladened limbs.

"Now, if you men could give me a hand to carry these in." Beatrice motioned to the full baskets sitting on the ground.

"Oh, sure. I'll just grab this basket." Franklin picked one up.

"It's a peck," said Beatrice.

"A what?"

"A peck."

"You, you mean like a kiss?" Franklin looked puzzled.

The whole group burst out laughing.

"Thems over there are bushels." Beatrice pointed at some other baskets.

Franklin stared blankly at Miki as if to say, *Is she for real?* "That's what a bushel and peck are?"

"Doris Day silly." Miki shook her head.

Nettie and Miki started singing a '50s song about a girl who loves her beau a bushel and a peck.

Oh no. It's happening again. Franklin rolled his eyes. There's always a weird song for everything. Who knew there would be one for a bushel and a peck?

"Oh, there's Granny," yelled North.

The frail old woman stood at the back screen door with an old shillelagh. Her thin skin made it easy to see every vein in her body.

"You can get them pecks and start picking since you drove all the way out here and don't seem to have anything to do," suggested Granny.

The five of them started casually picking cherries and joking with each other.

Beatrice said, "Just pull the berry with your fingers. If the cherry is ripe, the stem comes right off the tree."

Franklin tried it. "Oh, you're right."

"This is easy," said Miki.

"That's too bad," said Granny sarcastically.

"What do you do with them?" asked Franklin.

Beatrice answered, "We can them for pies."

Granny chuckled. "We carry them into the house." They all laughed, and she said, "You people laugh too much—do you ever get tired of laughing? Bring 'em into the sink," ordered Granny.

Inside, Franklin spied the farm kitchen sink. "Wow, now here's the real deal." He walked over and knocked on the sink with his knuckles. "This is cast iron. You know these are really in style now. Everyone in San Francisco is getting them." He looked up and down at the floor to ceiling cabinets made of bead board, and the table with seats for ten. "Yeah, they love this style." Gelatin molds of a rooster, pineapple, and a fish on the bead-board wall.

Beatrice asked, "Do they have many kids in a big city like San Francisco?"

"One or two." He studied the ceiling high cabinets. "Nice style."

"If you don't mind my asking, why do they need big cabinets? I don't think people in the big city do a lot of canning," said Granny.

Franklin shrugged. "People just like the farm kitchen look now."

"But they don't grow anything? So, they just look at it?"

"Uh-huh."

Granny rolled her eyes and turned to dump the cherries into the sink. "Are you going to help wash these cherries?"

"We're going out to pick more cherries, Granny," said Miki, and she followed Franklin out the back door.

"Well, don't dawdle. They won't pick themselves."

Miki and Franklin grabbed some more pecks and set them on a chair.

After an hour, Miki glanced at her watch. "I think we better get going to Elkport soon. The blacksmith is meeting us there."

They went back inside. Granny and North had dished up some cherry pie topped with whipping cream.

"Thanks for all your help. Preciate it," said Granny.

Chapter Thirty

GRANNY KELLER took Franklin, Miki, and the blacksmith to the back of the building with her coveted medieval key in hand. Once at the opening, she pointed out the ancient lock, still in its original place.

Franklin's eyes widened. "Unbelievable. That lock would have been stolen forty years ago in California."

Granny placed the key in the lock, turned it, and the door opened slightly, but they had to push it the rest of the way. Spiders scattered everywhere, but other than that, the iron didn't appear to have been touched for 100 years.

"Oh, heavens to Betsy," said Granny. "There's a lot here."

"Today, we'll identify and sort the equipment," said the blacksmith. "If there are things you don't need, I could use them in my shop"

"Go ahead and take it," said Granny.

"I'll have to come back tomorrow to finish the job."

"That's okay, just come back to Strawberry Bend and pick me up, and I'll bring the key."

"Are you kidding?" The blacksmith looked shocked.

Granny scowled. "No. I don't trust anybody with my lock and key. My grandfather brought it with him from Germany."

The blacksmith took the lock from her hand. "I have my own lock in the truck. This is handmade, you need to keep it. I would have it appraised."

After the blacksmith finished loading, they walked up to the general store. Miki pulled a few things from the building; some advertising plates, a match dispenser, and an old screen door.

"These would be cool for museum pieces."

They went back to the front of the building where North was working with a wooden frame with a heavy screen at the bottom. "This is a sifter," he explained. "Rocks back and forth, so the dirt will sift the treasures to the top."

The old lady's eyes lit up. "What did you find?"

"Well, Grandma, a lot of marbles!" North poured them out of a cloth bag sitting on the empty screen. "So far, five peewees, a bunch of core swirls." He held some up between his thumb and forefingers. "See the different core swirls. They're mostly red and green, some have solid core swirls with several bands of color in the middle and a clear space between each color, like this one. Aggies are made of agate."

"Well, those are all very pretty, but I have all my marbles," quipped Granny, and North laughed.

"It seems like marbles have existed forever, they're ubiquitous," said Franklin. "The Greeks, Romans, and Egyptians all had them. Some of the oldest marbles are made of clay. That must be what your marbles are made of Granny," North quipped.

Granny laughed. "You're right on that one."

"These core swirls over here became popular in the early 1800s," said North. "They were invented by a glassblower from Germany who could make them very cheap because he came up with a special scissor to cut molten glass. Can you imagine how the Germans around here wanted marbles from the home country? Look, here's a blizzard—all the colors spin around in a circle in a clear marble. I saw one sold for ten thousand dollars recently."

"Oh my gosh." Granny stared wide-eyed from her Coke bottle glasses. "That's a lot of money."

"Great! One more display for the museum. Finds from a ghost town." Miki clapped her hands together.

"I also found five solid silver coins, and there is a whole pile of horseshoes buried over there next to the blacksmith shop."

"Those are sad looking horseshoes. They're all bent," said Nettie.

"Yeah, see these nails," said North. "These are the ones the farrier pulled off the horse when they wear down. Mostly rusted into the soil now. They're so bent. But the most interesting thing I found was in front of the church. It was a little rusted ring box."

"Do tell," said Miki.

"When I opened the box, an earwig crawled out, and it fell apart in my hand. Inside was a solitaire ring in mud. It has a dark blue stone, a sapphire I guess."

"Wouldn't you like to know the story about that?" Miki's eyes widened.

North pulled the ring out of the change pocket in his jeans and then poured some bottled water over it.

Nettie struggled to contain her emotions. Words were screaming from the bottom of her lungs.

North held the ring out for Miki to slip on her finger. "Here, try it on."

"It fits perfectly," said Miki and slipped it on her ring finger.

"Well, why don't you keep it for all the work you're doing here."

Nettie swallowed hard. A ghost from her past punched her in the gut. She wanted to see the ring but said nothing.

Chapter Thirty-One

THE NEXT DAY, a heavy-duty truck with a lift pulled up to the blacksmith shop. He identified the pieces he wanted to set up for a display. Volunteers helped Miki and North load the iron equipment onto the truck.

Nettie drove into Elkport. She stopped halfway down the street, got out of her car, and stared at the nearly collapsing Victorian. Vines climbed inside the broken windows and up to the roof, and grass was peeking through the porch boards.

She turned around when a car pulled in behind her.

"Nettie, is that you?"

It was the sheriff.

"Hi, Marty."

"I got a call some people were over here. I might have known you were the instigator."

"No. I'm the distraction while they steal the jewels out the back door. It seems to be working."

"You got that right."

"North has a permit to get the blacksmith equipment and do some excavating. We're creating a new museum in Elkton."

"Ahh. I'll have to get up there to see it when you're done. I'm retiring the end of November."

"We're getting old, Grandpa Marty."

"Getting a last look at your old house?"

"Uh-huh."

"Thinking about the two trees? We had a lot of fun with Old Glory and Tammy. Those are the kind of pets that go to heaven. They'll be there."

"Yes."

"The house will be gone, Nettie, but those trees aren't going anywhere. They'll be here forever." He started back the car. "Oh, I have a surprise for you."

"Really?"

"Yeah, it's a Christmas present. Something we did together when we were wee ones."

"What?" They both laughed.

"I'm not telling. It will ruin the surprise. I heard you made a replica of our church."

Nettie looked at the church. "A lot of memories there of you and Caleb. Nobody remembers him now much. Been gone a long time."

He looked at her and paused. "He showed me the ring."

She looked directly into his eyes.

"He was so happy. He loved you more than I've seen anyone love a girl. We were all running away from marriage, and he was running to it. You were a pretty Iowa girl, a real catch. I was jealous."

Nettie's eyes widened. "Marty. Thanks for remembering."

"Thanks for leaving a piece of cake on the tombstone."

"Oh, come on."

"Just kidding, it was mostly gone when I got there."

They both chuckled.

"I miss my brother." Marty smiled but then said, "Hey, I want one of them lighted houses for my Christmas present if you got one. I've got every piece you made of Christmasville. It's something to hold onto. Next year, make a house with me in front with a big smile."

Marty put his hand on the steering wheel, and the Nettie noticed the sun glistened off his wedding ring.

"I've never been unhappy with Aggie," said Marty. "You know why? She's just like you."

Nettie smiled. "Thank you, my childhood friend."

She reluctantly waved good-bye as Marty drove around back.

Chapter Thirty-Two

Nettie slowly approached the little wooden church at the end of the street. She stared at it a long time from the car.

"Well, I've replicated you, old church. We won't forget how well you served us. I'll miss you perfectly perched above Elkport."

She walked up the stairs and opened the door to the little church. She stepped inside. The rope for the bell still in the same place, and she gently took it in her hand.

She paused but only briefly.

Oh, what the heck.

She pulled down with all her strength to make the heavy bell ring. The bell pealed brilliantly, and she pulled three times until she was exhausted.

She walked into the chapel and looked at the pews she and her friends used to sit in. She sat down and looked at the altar.

Nettie felt like her heart would burst thinking of her friends in Sunday School.

The first farmers in this area lived and died passing within your walls. Goodbye, my old friend. I am getting old, but there is still much to do. I feel like I could go on forever.

She closed the doors one last time and stared at the steps.

"Mom?"

Startled, Nettie looked up.

"I heard you guys were out here scavenging." Noel hugged her mom's shoulders.

Nettie opened her purse and pulled out the picture of her and Caleb as children sitting on some steps.

Miki joined them and studied the picture. "The steps in the picture are these same steps? I had no idea, Grandma."

Nettie sighed. "Yes, we were so young and carefree. The whole world was ours for the taking. We were inseparable."

"What happened to your beau, Mom? You mention him now and then. I'm afraid to ask because I think it will make you sad."

"No. It's been a long time now. I'm sorry you felt you couldn't talk to me about it."

"I've seen you out at the cemetery, Grandma. I know you go regularly. You never married," said Miki

"I was eighteen, and Caleb was twenty. We always knew we would marry. Our parents used to joke after God made us two, he threw away the mold. We were born for each other. I guess no one ever matched up to Caleb. I didn't intend to *not* marry. I just never found anyone. After a while, I decided that was the answer. I always wanted children, so I decided to adopt. I went to an orphanage, and I saw you, and you climbed up in my lap. You were my daughter, and I stopped looking. Best decision I ever made."

Nettie put her arm around Noel's waist. "You were only two with auburn hair and freckles. Those bright blue eyes and long eye lashes. You smiled at me as if to say, here I am, take me home, Mom. What's not to love here?'"

Noel burst into tears. "You never told me that before, Mom."

Nettie hugged her daughter.

"How did Caleb die?" asked Noel. "What happened to him, Mom? I went to look at his stone one time after you left. He died in 1957. Was it a tractor accident?"

"Let's sit on this bench. My back is tired." Nettie put her arm around Noel.

"No, it wasn't a tractor. Rain was predicted for Northeastern Iowa that day but to the north of us. I was working in the corn fields with Papa, and we never heard the news. It was sunny where we were, and the bluffs blocked the view of the horizon."

Nettie's thoughts drifted thinking about Elkport. "We had a crèche in front of the altar every year. It was carved in 1860 by an early German pioneer. The one North is working on with his dad.

"How he labored to restore it. With a profusion of color, he brought the whole set to life. His gift was mixing colors, he was like Rembrandt. When I think of what masterpieces he could have made in his life, it breaks my heart. I guess he's just been making heaven beautiful all these years. I like to think of him that way. Content.

"I was supposed to meet him that afternoon after my chores. He had a surprise for me, a ring. Without a care in the world, I mounted Old Glory and started making my way through the woods winding down to the valley floor. For a second, a thought I heard an unusual sound like a water-logged freight train that was bearing down. It wasn't my imagination. I had a front row seat for the worst tragedy in our valley's history. Trains were thrown off their tracks. I kicked Glory, fearing we were living our last moments, but she reared, and I nearly slipped off her back. She was slipping and stumbling on the loose rock. We moved sideways, and the horse slipped to her knees and groaned in pain. I decided to dismount, but I turned to see water flood the whole valley, and a barn was grabbed, and it was smashed against some boulders and quickly shattered apart. All at once Glory surged up the hill with the water rising at our heels.

"I realized that Caleb could have been standing in front of church waiting for me to give me my engagement ring. Was the church still there? I was sick with worry. I could see the altered tree line, and the steeple poking through. It was still there. I prayed to God to please let him be inside the church. At least it was still standing.

"It was getting late, and there was no movement or calls for help. After several men tried to slug their way through waist deep mud filled with debris, it was decided to call them off until sunrise.

"The next day, people went out to examine the damage and tried to figure out who was missing. The church was still upright, but no sign of a living thing. The church door was unlocked, step risers and treads were ripped from the string on one side. In the church, there were only paint brushes with paint on them. His palette upside down on the floor and carpentry tools on the attic worktable where Caleb had been. He must have panicked. The minister pulled one of the searchers aside away from me. He whispered, 'Caleb must have been out on the landing when the wooden stairs were washed away.' I heard him and thought the same thing. They started the work we dreaded, to find the eleven missing people in the mud. I was instructed to go home, and Caleb and two children weren't found for three days. They were two miles downstream caught within some boulders and trees and packed in mud. The carving of Jesus was nearby with the arms broken off on top of some debris. Some thought he stuffed it down his shirt to help keep him afloat. I was *so* angry. We would never be married. I felt like I was sleepwalking. It just couldn't be real. The man I loved was now in a cemetery. The only way I could talk to him was standing in front of a cold stone. I would never hear his voice again in this life."

"Mom, that's such a hard thing to deal with anytime, but especially at eighteen." Noel hugged her mother, and tears ran down their faces. "We're glad you told us now."

For the first time, Nettie grieved Caleb's death and her deepest secrets and losses with her daughter and granddaughter.

"I'm so sorry," said Miki. "It happened in this valley that you loved, with all the happy memories as children. He could have been the grandfather I never had. That's a weird thought. For the first time, I just realized that *I* lost something that day," she said thoughtfully.

Franklin and North walked up.

"We need to get this stuff down to the museum. It's getting late," said Franklin.

Both men stopped, turned, and walked away, looking embarrassed. They had interupted the women in a private moment.

Shortly thereafter, the three women walked down to the car to meet them.

Nettie looked back, and in her mind, she saw Caleb standing in front of the nativity, and it warmed her heart.

Chapter Thirty-Three

FRANKLIN AND MIKI looked over the Main Street Alive plans. "I talked to Dingle. I noticed that you were over at the site when the farmhouse was lifted and moved to another location. I talked with him about it, and we decided to save it."

"So, he's including you in the decisions now?"

"Yeah." Franklin looked pleased with himself. "Can you believe it? We're going to develop another lot next door just for the Victorian farmhouse."

"I've always loved the old Williams farmhouse, with the steep roof and unique gingerbread on the outside. The woodwork on the inside is fabulous, too. I remember going in there one time for trick or treating. I think it had a Swiss architect." Miki suddenly gave Franklin a brief hug. "I'm so happy, Lin. You're becoming a huge asset around here."

Franklin grinned. "I know Dingle was planning on selecting the name himself for the subdivision. I suggested something a long time ago, and he liked it. Eagle Nest Country Estates. The streets will be names of Iowa birds."

"That's a great idea." Miki clapped her hands.

"Not only that, but we also talked about having a recreation room in the middle lot with some basketball hoops to give the kids a place to meet and be closer to home. Family friendly."

"Are you kidding? Mr. Dingle is turning into a real all-star."

Franklin shrugged. "It's a miracle. I guess he's not as bad as we thought he was."

Miki and Franklin picked up two hardhats and walked onsite.

"These will be wonderful startup homes," said Miki. "They're needed so desperately. How many bedrooms?"

"Three bedrooms and one and a half bathrooms. Twelve hundred and seventy-five square feet. They'll each have a fireplace and a laundry room with a mud sink," said Franklin.

"I love a mud sink. Not just for gardening but for cleaning paint brushes."

Franklin looked at her quizzically.

"Just being practical." She laughed. "These houses are a great design, that's all I'm saying."

"It's supposed to rain all week, is everyone taking a week off?"

"I think so," said Miki. Then she added, "I love the gingerbread that's going up and the restored woodwork. The new signs really make an impression. Uncle Woot brought his rotor saw, and I think the kids learned some skills, too."

"They did a nice job. They made this whole street seem like home. By the way, my parents said they would like to come out here to visit."

"Really? It would be nice to meet them."

"Yeah, they would like to meet you, too."

"So, Nate Williams is bringing the garret, windmill, and water tower over tomorrow. They put the foundations in last month. This is really going to be an amazing museum."

"It's such a beautiful day, I would like to take a trip down to Dubuque to go sightseeing. Let's go to Eagle Point Park this time. I want to take some pictures in summer and send them to my parents."

Miki and Franklin stopped by Nettie's and let her know they were going down to Dubuque for the day.

"Cleveland Park is beautiful." Miki sat on a bench, and Franklin sat next to her. They could see the river and downtown.

"What do you suppose is on those barges?"

"Could be a lot of things. Food, fuel? Your parents are interested in these pictures?"

"I always share my trips with them."

"Sounds like you are very close."

"Yes, we are," said Franklin. "My parents are old-fashioned, and they brought us up that way. I'm glad, although we were a bit odd in the city by the bay."

Franklin snapped a couple of pictures. "Okay, I got what I need here. Except, I'd like one with you by the bridge. Maybe we could go down to the riverfront and the tower later. I want to see Julien Dubuque's grave again." He jotted down a few notes on his tablet of what he wanted to take pictures of for his parents.

They drove down Grandview Avenue, a lovely street with islands in the middle filled with brightly colored flowers. At another time of year, the same islands had Peony bushes.

"The flowers have the most heavenly scent," said Miki.

They turned down to a valley, crossed over to another bluff, and ascended into a miniature forest. Once at the top, they parked and walked out to the monument where the most incredible view of the Mississippi River extended north and south. The tall cylinder topped with a castellated trim, was totally made of buff limestone blocks.

Miki explained. "Originally, the Indians faced his grave to the south because it was his favorite view over the river. It was their tradition to build a little house on top of the grave. And bury the body sitting up partially out of the ground, so he had a view. When the Native Americans buried a young warrior, they would kill his horse and bury it with him."

"What a shame."

"I know, I love horses. From their point a view, death is a journey, and a warrior doesn't really die, he just begins a new journey to the Great Spirit. It can take a month to get there. I thought that was a beautiful concept.

"Once the body is consumed by nature, they rebury the bones."

"It makes sense because it's a journey."

"In the late 1800s, someone claimed they took Julien's jawbone. Citizens became concerned. So, they dug up the skeleton and discovered a female on top of his skeleton. Presumed to be his Indian wife Potosa. She was the daughter of Chief Peosta. and his grave is back there to the west."

"So, this monument was built to protect a grave?" asked Franklin as they looked at the river. "This place looks so verdant and lush like the Garden of Eden might have been."

"So, we don't know much about the love story, except that it happened here." Miki's hands were in her pockets as she looked down on Catfish Creek and the flat land where the Mesquakie lived.

Franklin snapped a picture of Miki.

I think I'm falling in love with this woman. She really thinks about the world around her. I never want to forget this moment.

He took another picture of her in front of the monument from the west with the sunset on her face. The golden pink hues reflected off her hair and clothes, and she seemed to sparkle like a gem in a perfect setting.

"Down below here to the right was the Mesquakie village near Catfish Creek. They lived in elongated bark lodges. This area is called the Mines of Spain. Can't you imagine them there?"

"This really has been amazing," said Franklin. He stretched his back. "I can drive if you like."

"Sure. Let's get a hamburger and a root beer float at the A&W for the road."

"Okay, I would really like to get a picture of the island tower in that valley by Durango if there's time."

"We used to go horseback riding down there. The Double D Ranch I think they called it. In the fall, that tower has red sumac on it, and it's so beautiful."

"Maybe in the fall if I'm here."

"You don't think you will be here?" Miki looked over at him.

Franklin turned up the radio and sang along with "Born in the USA".

Chapter Thirty-Four

"I CAN SEE WHY you have such a fondness for this community. I went to the antique gas station yesterday and was treated to a free oil check and a window wash. I've heard about that. I never expected it to happen." Franklin's eyes widened.

"Nice, huh?"

"Yeppers."

"I'm so excited. It's really all going to happen, Lin. What will we do for all the volunteers? We need a thank you party."

Miki started to search her phone for ideas and prices for banners of light to go across Main Street.

"I was so busy at the museum and the garret today. By the way, it's mounted and bolted down, but I forgot to put a couple Christmas decoration proposals together for the town council tonight. Let's get over to the office."

Chapter Thirty-Five

IT'S THE LAST WEEK of June, most of the buildings are in the process of being painted, volunteers and laborers are downtown. They are using sprayers, rollers, and still others painting the front trim with brushes.

The smell of paint filled the air, and hammers, aluminum ladders, and scaffolding contributed to the sound of the construction as each building transformed from an ugly duckling to a lady of Victorian distinction.

The building near the museum was painted brick red with cream windows and face boards along the roof. The gingerbread and porch trim were medium seaport blue, and a white picket fence spanned the front, giving it a patriotic look. In the center of the yard was a homemade wishing well bird bath and feeder.

Someone donated faux iron plant holders for the insides of the porch columns, and several ladies had been growing pots of flowers.

A second Victorian in the Queen Anne style was lilac violet with white trim and goldenrod details. Several half barrels lined the sidewalk and were overflowing with African Impatience, with the shade of an oak tree near the sidewalk's end.

Another home painted basic white by the owners with a lovely petunia pink trim. Uncle Woot made a Genova Gable decoration with elegant, ornate curves.

Profuse pink and purple petunias decorated a short two-foot fence along the front.

The last business was a brick Italianate that had several fill-ins of a more modern brick, so they decided to paint it. They chose moss green with a trim called straw to brighten up the entire building.

Electrical outlets were installed for the Christmas lights, and new street signs added to the scene. Black and white signs distinguished each store and the museum, and at each end of Main Street, a wood carved black and white sign that read:

Welcome to Old Towne Elkton
The biggest little town around

Miki stared at the ugly decrepit bank building right in the middle of it all.

"I feel like I failed the Richardsonian wreck."

Franklin shook his head. "I disagree. It's still summer, so there's hope. Have faith."

"I do, but that ugly for sale sign really draws attention to it."

"Oh, come on droopy-drawers." Franklin teased.

"Droopy drawers?"

"Well, it got a smile on your face."

Miki continued. "It was made of red sandstone brought all the way from an Arizona quarry. Those two symmetrical sandstone rails sweep out making each step two feet wider than the step above it. People must feel their bank is solid and substantial if you want them to put their money inside. Those original hanging gas lamps inside must be worth some money. I'll have to see if I can find a picture of the bank when it was new to peak the interest of a buyer."

"Let's walk down to the grocery store and get something to eat," said Franklin.

As they walked past the stores, Miki yelled to the owner of the Italianate, "I love the colors. So much better."

The owner smiled. "I'm glad you told me. I was feeling a little dubious."

"It needed to be brightened. Very welcoming now."

Miki was surprised to see the Piggly Bigly had a new look as well. The picture windows glistened, the brick below the windows had been cleaned and painted, and it appeared they had steam cleaned the front sidewalk.

"They added a vestibule to the corner door. That's nice, it will keep it warmer in the winter."

Later that day, Miki, Franklin, North, and Nettie met at the museum.

Nettie held a piece of paper in her hand. "Hey, on the Fourth of July weekend, let's take a field trip. At the county courthouse, I found the location of John Schweikert's farm along the Turkey River. "

"Grandma, where's he buried?" asked Miki.

"In Garber just the other side of the river from Elkport," said Nettie. "When we have the time, I'll take you down to the private cemetery."

"I'd like to go to Spillville," said North.

"Great, I'd like to go there. You know, all the time I've lived here, I've wanted to go, but I never have," said Miki.

North walked up behind them. "Dvorak wrote the New World Symphony while over-looking the town. I've been there three times." He stood still for several seconds. "Uh, do you guys need any help?"

No one responded.

North left and walked back to his truck.

Nettie hurried after him. "North, where are you going?"

"Well, I was feeling a little like a third wheel over there."

Nettie quickly glanced back toward the museum, then back to North. "Hmmm, well no need to feel that way. I'm sure they didn't hear you. Next Sunday, we are going on a little field trip, I want you to go with us."

"Okay," he paused for a second, "if *you* want me to go."

On July 5, everyone going on the field trip piled into Noel's black SUV. Nettie came armed with a map, stories, and a CD of K-Tel's greatest novelty songs. To the dismay of Franklin and North all three of the ladies amused themselves by singing about their favorite cowgirl. There's a showdown and half the town gets shot to H-E-double hockey sticks.

North and Franklin stared at each other from opposite sides of the back seat. North shook his head in disbelief.

Franklin whispered, "Are there any other CDs in this car?"

North shrugged. "Let's ask her to tell us another story, she loves those."

Franklin nodded.

"Nettie," began North, "why don't you tell us about your ancestor John before we get there. We might think of some questions."

"Good idea, North. I've never been there myself. But I have some pictures of the barn that they lived in."

Franklin asked, "Are…are you saying your ancestors lived in a barn?"

Nettie nodded. "Yes, they did. They were very poor, you know. John had sixteen children."

"They must have been really bored in the old days," mumbled Franklin.

"Sixteen kids?" Miki glared at Franklin.

Nettie looked back at North who was laughing.

Nettie continued. "There were two wives, though. His first wife, Wilhemina, died in childbirth. She was birthing our great-grandmother, Charlotte. So, we're lucky, none of us would have been here."

"And the second wife?" asked Miki.

"He met Angelina Lewis in a general store in Ohio. She was twenty years younger than him. They just looked at each other and knew. With eight kids he needed a wife."

Franklin looked out the window. "This green countryside must have looked like heaven to John, the soil is so black."

"Nah, it's just Iowa." Miki smiled.

"*The Field of Dreams* again. Hey, isn't that baseball field around here?" asked Franklin.

"Yes, it's out passed Dyersville. About forty minutes away," said Noel.

"I could take you if you want. I played catch with my dad there. One of my fondest memories with him. You don't have to say anything. Just throw. You learn more about someone when you're quiet," said Miki.

"Would you like to see a picture of John and Angelina's wedding?"

"Sure." North reached for the picture. "You just happened to have that with you?"

"Smell that cow manure and check out the hogs." Noel laughed. "We get the combo package today."

"Cool tractors, they have yellow and green," said Franklin.

"The corn is still pretty short," said Noel. "As the saying goes, knee high by the fourth of July."

Nettie stared at an old white barn at the back of the property. "I can't believe it, it's still here."

Transfixed, she climbed out of the car and walked through a gate of the small farmhouse.

Nettie knocked on the door and waited. A woman came to the door. "Can I help you?"

"Hi, my name is Nettie Holmes, my great-grandfather John Schweikert used to own this property way back in 1857." She showed her the pictures. "I wondered if we could look at the barn?"

The woman looked at the picture. "I'm Alice Krapfl," she said and turned to a boy. "Can you go get your dad?"

A man came to the door.

"Karl, this is Nettie. She wants to look at the barn." Alice handed him the picture. "Her ancestor used to own this property."

Karl's eyebrows rose. "You don't say! This is their wedding picture?"

Nettie nodded. "Yes, he had sixteen children and two wives, and they lived in the barn out back."

"Here is a picture of four of their children. They came back in their old age to see if the house was still there."

Alice gasped. "They lived there?"

"Yes, they came back in, I believe, 1950. They found their mother's spinning wheel and John's beaver skin top hat. They were still up in the loft."

Karl said, "In the loft in that barn?" He laughed. "Well, you're welcome to go out there and take some pictures."

They went through the back yard and across the field to the barn.

When inside, Nettie studied the old 1850's barn. "We're so spoiled with all our conveniences. How did they survive in the cold? And raise children here?" She sighed. "When I think of all the years I spent trying to figure out their journey."

"I can't believe they lived here," Noel said.

Miki put her arm around Nettie. "How do you feel, Grandma?"

Nettie sighed. "Happy and melancholy."

They walked outside. Franklin chuckled and said to North, "Hey, you forgot to shut the door, were your ancestors born in a barn?"

Nettie walked along the river next to the cornfield, and Franklin took her picture.

Nettie looked across the field. "You wonder what secrets they might have had. We were told that John came across the ocean from Germany smuggled in a hogshead; but was he? No, I found his passenger list and he came over with his siblings. So many families have the same story, who knows which ones are true.

"We do know that during the 1849 gold rush, he considered going to California, but when people wrote back to Iowa, they told him not to go. They said it's very hard, that people can steal or even kill to get your gold. John didn't go, but he did go to Australia when gold was discovered there. All he found was a small piece of gold, so he came back. He later had that gold made into a wedding ring for Angelina."

"Where is the ring, Grandma?" asked Miki.

"I understand one of our relatives in Texas has it." She put her arm around Miki and Noel. "I never would have done this little trip by myself. Thanks for coming with me."

Menacing clouds gathered overhead. The air was perfectly calm, even the birds stopped chirping.

"It's suddenly so calm," said Miki.

"Yeah, it is," agreed North

"Check out that sky, the clouds are so black. We don't have many thunderstorms in California," said Franklin.

In seconds, the weather had changed drastically. Streaks of lightening shot out of thick rolling black clouds followed by fierce winds and loud claps of thunder.

They all ran for the barn.

"Is this a tornado?" Franklin was freaking out.

Thunder rocked the barn; the lightening and thunder were non-stop.

Something crashed into the side of the barn.

"I wonder what *that* was?" said Miki.

"Let's sit on the ground," said Nettie, and she looked up. "I sure hope they have lightning rods on the roof."

The door was open. They saw a lightning bolt hit a piece of rebar. It flew up in the air and crashed back to the ground with an awful thud.

"That could have been us," yelled Franklin.

They all held hands and prayed for protection.

Soon the storm crossed the river and left as fast as it had come.

Franklin took a deep breath. "Okay, that was scary. I've never been more frightened in my entire life, or more grateful for this barn. We could have been killed out there."

They walked outside to a perfectly calm, blue sky. A beautiful rainbow appeared in the sky, and Franklin started taking pictures again. He pointed at the clouds. "Does that look like a stairway to anyone else?"

"It seems like a sign," said Nettie. "Maybe our ancestors know we're thinking of them."

"It really does look like a stairway going up to heaven," said Noel.

"And the clouds look golden. It's so weird," said North.

"I'm starting to understand the genealogy stuff, Nettie," said Franklin.

"Kinda feels like deja vu," said Miki, thoughtfully.

"What does that mean, Miki?"

Miki said, "Before I left Chicago in November, I dreamed that there was a stairway to heaven. Then I dreamed of a little wooden church with a large moon behind its steeple. Something was flying in the air. When Franklin and I first got here, we saw the Elkport church in the moonlight.

"When I saw the church and I thought of that dream, I figured that was what it was about. Usually, I can figure out my dreams, but it made no sense to me. It had nothing to do with *my* life." She shrugged.

The group returned to Garber and to the cemetery where John, Angelina, and Wilhelmina were buried.

The entrance was protected by a metal fence and gate with a banner over the top with the cemetery name on.

HANSEL CEMETERY

Inside the gate stood a tall black stone.

They stood there, and no one talked.

"It makes you think about your own life, and how you're living it," said Nettie.

Miki wrote in her journal later that night.

We came home different people. We shared a sacred experience together.

Chapter Thirty-Six

MONDAY AFTERNOON Miki noticed the absence of the for sale sign in front of the bank.

The mayor approached her. "Congratulations, Miki!"

"On what?" she said, quizzically.

"You found a buyer for the old bank."

"I did?"

Franklin walked up to them. "You're so modest, Miki. Wonder what the new owners will do with it."

The mayor continued. "You two are the best team, don't listen to any naysayers. You're both so devoted to this project, working all these months on the museum. Your grandma donating her talents, which are many. The new school program is amazing. The costumes that you made are wonderful. What a lifetime memory you're going to give the children."

"Thank you, mayor."

He walked away quickly. "And congratulations once again."

Miki looked at Franklin. "But I didn't get the bank sold."

Franklin waved at the mayor, and Miki said, "I seriously don't know what he's talking about."

"I guess it's a mystery then."

Just then a truck from a sandblasting company pulled up in front of the bank.

"Somebody did buy it. How did this happen?" asked Miki.

"Well…did I tell you my parents arrived this morning?"

"No."

"My parents came to see the Williams' old farmhouse, and they love it. And then they took my brother and sister to see the bank, and they both loved that."

"Your parents bought them? Wow. Why would they do that?"

"They wanted to find a place to retire."

"In Iowa?"

"I sent them all those pictures, and they loved what they saw."

"No way. What will they do with the bank, rent it?"

"My brother and sister have some learning disabilities. My parents decided to buy the bank and turn it into apartments for them. They'll only be a couple blocks away, so Mom and Dad can check up on them. Lincoln and Madison like to be independent."

"That's cool, wait. You have a brother named Lincoln and a sister named Madison?"

"What can I say, my parents are patriotic? It's a wacky tradition that's been going on in my dad's line for generations."

Miki looked past Franklin to four people walking toward them.

"I've told them all about you. They can't wait to meet you, Miki."

"Guess I don't know why they would want to live here."

"I understand. Guess I never told you. My mom is from Mason City, and we grew up with the *Music Man*, morning, noon, and night. It's my siblings' favorite. It's just a *thing* in my family. Mom just retired after being a music director at a junior college. When I told her about the farmhouse, she had to come see it. It reminds her of her grandmother's house. In San Francisco, we always have our own Special Olympics in our backyard. They'll have a bigger yard now."

"Wow, I had no idea."

The four people approached Franklin and Miki.

Lincoln and Madison ran up to Franklin, obviously elated to see their brother.

In pure Madison fashioned, she took Miki's hand. "I love you," she said.

Miki looked directly into Madison's eyes and smiled.

"Hi, Miki," said Franklin's mother.

"Miki, this is my mom, Janet," said Franklin.

"Nice to meet you, Miki. Looky what I have." She held up an old-fashioned key. "Let's go make some plans." She opened the door to the old bank.

Janet started singing about all the brass instruments gleaming in the sun. She linked arms with her daughter, and they marched together and paraded into the bank.

Franklin grabbed Madison's arm and they burst out into song describing the exaggerated numbers of youth marching in enthusiasm.

Lincoln followed, "Rows and rows of virch-os." Because he can't pronounce virtuosos. And happily, he marches in the old bank building, soon to be his home.

Shocked, Miki stared after them as a dignified man in his fifty's approached her

"I'm Garfield, and I assume you're Miki? If you don't make any remarks about me having a teddy bear named Pookie, we'll be great friends. Call me Gary, for short."

Franklin, Madison, Janet, and Lincoln were still singing inside.

Hearing the singing, Garfield laughed and said to Miki, "I don't really get it either. But they're *so happy*. Shall we join them?"

He held out his arm for Miki. She took it, and they joined the others inside.

Chapter Thirty-Seven

FRANKLIN WALKED toward the bakery, and Miki stepped out of the door.

"Would you like a Danish? Custard, your favorite."

"How would you know that?" Franklin reached for the custard.

"I remembered from Galena."

"No secrets around here. '*It's the biggest little town around.*"

"Ha-ha."

Miki took a bite of the Danish.

"I'm going to Dubuque. Grandma asked me to drop off some papers to Joe and then go see Mom. One of her ladies passed."

"Can I go with you? I'd love to get some photos from Dubuque's Grave in summer."

"Sure, I'd enjoy the company."

"You're really close to your family."

"Yea, we're tight. Someday, I'll have to look after my brother and sister."

"That's very sweet of you, Linny."

"Linny?" Franklin's eyebrows shot up.

She laughed. "I like your parents, too."

"Miki, Miki!" called Nettie, as she walked up to them pulling a red wagon filled with stuff. "Here's the items for Joe. They belonged to Caleb's grandfather. He purchased a Holland sleigh that had a large H on the front. These are the advertisements from the factory. They show all the different sleighs they made in the 1890's. Some double seaters, and four or six seaters."

"Grandma, this is amazing."

"I thought he might want to blow them up and frame them for the walls of his museum." She held up a robe. "Also, here are a couple accoutrements. A buffalo robe and this." She held up a long leather whip.

"Oh my gosh. Where did you get these?"

Franklin took the robe. "I want to try it." He snapped the whip.

"Wow, that's loud. Have you done that before?"

"Nope. It's fun, but it seems harsh to whip the horse with this."

"You don't whip the horse. You just crack it at his side," explained Nettie.

"Anyway, tell him they belonged to Caleb's parents. The family let me take what I wanted after they passed."

"They must have really loved you, Grandma."

"Yes, they did. Oh, and this." Nettie handed Miki a large rectangular box.

"What is it?"

"The plume is for the horse's head. Isn't that the bomb?"

Miki and Franklin did a double take at Nettie and glanced at each other.

"What?" said Miki.

"They've been using that slang since the forties. We weren't just Elkport bumpkins, you know."

Nettie held the plume out and let the feathers move with the breeze.

Nettie's mind drifted away. "I'll tell you a funny story. It was 1937, and I was in pigtail braids and a gingham dress, and I picked up the receiver of the wall phone. It was Caleb, and he told me to get over there right now cause his dad had gone crazy, that he took Grandpa's sleigh, hooked up to a horse, said they were going to church in it.

"Mom yelled for me to hang up, and I dropped the receiver, so it was hanging there with Caleb talking to no one. Mom came in the kitchen and could hear a scratchy voice. She picked up the receiver and said, 'Caleb E. Hammel, is that you? I'm going to tell your mama your wasting time on the phone,' and she hung it up.

"I ran through the snow across the harvested corn field. When I got there, the barn door flew open, and Mr. Hammel rode out in a sleigh. I was just in time to see Caleb's mom run outside and see the sleigh complete with bells and a large red circus plume on the horse's head.

"Mr. Hammel yelled, 'When I was a little boy, my grandpa used to take me riding to church in this on Christmas.' His wife was yelling, 'It's freezing out here. I'm not riding in this. It's 1937, I want to ride to church in a car!'

"Caleb was arguing that it was fun, and his sister that it was a surprise for their mom, but she just folded her arms saying she wouldn't do it. Caleb, Marty and his sister kept begging, and finally, their mom got in the sleigh, and so did I. We each pulled out a buffalo hide and wrapped it around us to keep warm.

"The bells sounded so pretty, and Mr. Hammel was having so much fun. We all started singing, 'God Bless Ye Merry Gentleman.' I looked over at Mrs. Mattie—she was singing heartily and pulled her buffalo robe to her cheeks. I looked at Caleb, Marty and his sister, and I could see we all felt the same, all because of Caleb's father.

"When we pulled up to the front of the church, everyone came running out to greet us. They all wanted a ride. We were so popular that day. I'll never forget the look of absolute joy on Mr. Hammel's face. He told the boys to throw the buffalo hides over the horse's back while he tied the reins to the handrail, and the whole congregation walked us in. Marty hitched a ride back with us on the floor of the sleigh, and then we took Mrs. Mattie home. We spent two and a half hours giving rides to every kid, young and old, all around town. Sometimes over frozen corn fields to be rebels, until we went over a small snowbank, and I now understood the line. 'And wee, we got up sot.' Scary."

While Nettie was remembering her childhood, Miki turned the plume upside down. "And there it is, Holland Sleigh Co. 1892." She looked over to her grandma.

Nettie had her eyes closed, but she smiled and started singing to herself, "God Rest Ye Merry Gentlemen let…" She opened her eyes, and the smile melted off her face when she realized she was singing a Christmas carol in July.

"Are you okay, Grandma?"

"Sure, sure. Just remembering." Nettie paused. "You know, there was always a rumor when I was little about Holland Sleighs. They said that old man Holland built one on Christmas Eve, and that it had special powers."

Miki was quiet for a second. "Well, that seems a little silly. Too hard to believe."

"I suppose." She sighed. "Well, have a safe trip and say hi to your mother."

Chapter Thirty-Eight

WHEN THEY ARRIVED in Dubuque, they took the items to Joe. He was surprised and glad to have them. When they got to Noel's house, Miki found her mother pacing the floor and emotionally spent.

"Mom, I'm so sorry." Miki hugged her. "I'm sorry about your patient."

"I can't get the image of her out of my mind. I knew something was wrong when the front door was open. She never does that, and her dogs were stressed and hungry. When I finally got to a back bedroom, she was dead on the floor without her walker. Why didn't she have her walker? She must have been disoriented and perhaps in a lot of pain. I wasn't there to help her." Noel cried, "She must have been scared. Hannah might still be alive if I had come earlier."

"*That* has to be so hard, Mom." Miki rubbed her mother's shoulders.

"No one should die alone. It's the one thing we're all scared of, isn't it. To not have someone we love by our side. I've been taking care of her for over three and a half years."

"Her family is there now, right?"

Noel wiped her eyes. "Yes."

"It's not your fault she died alone, Mom. She could have lost consciousness and maybe didn't know she was alone. But no matter, you know she appreciated all the times you've been there for her. I understand you're sad, but it wasn't your fault in any way. There's no way to fix it."

Miki said to her mom, "We're going out to Julien Dubuque's grave. Why don't you come with us. You can get out of the house for a while and see the world from a different point of view."

"Yeah, come with us," said Franklin. "That's a great idea."

"I don't want to, but I think you're right. I think I will go."

They stopped by a florist, and Miki ran in, grabbed a box of rose petals, and then they drove straight to the grave.

At the block, they sat on a bench overlooking the mile-wide river.

"Mom, why don't you tell us why you're grateful to have known your friend, and we'll throw some rose petals to honor her."

Soon, there were multicolored petals all over the ground, and Franklin took a picture of Noel and Miki sitting on the bench, her arm around her mom.

"I know someone who had the weight of the world on his shoulders, Black Hawk," Miki said quietly.

"You mean from the Black Hawk War?" Noel said.

"Yeah, it's what happened to him after he left the Wisconsin River near the bluffs. The Indians had no ability to do anything but retreat, so they wouldn't all be killed. Literally, they buried their axes along the hills before they got in the river. They hoped the army would stop chasing them, and they were stalling in the highlands, so the women and children could escape down river.

"Eventually, they ended up at a place we call Bad Axe in Wisconsin on the river front. They were surprised to find a boat loaded with cannons that started shooting at them. They struggled to swim across the Mississippi River to get back to Iowa.

"The Winnebago, it is thought, secreted Black Hawk away to perform rituals for his surrender. Basically, to wear sackcloth and ashes in humility for leading his people to this fate. The last step was to dress in white deerskin, so all could see him and know he was humbled. He turned himself in, and Jefferson Davis was assigned to take him to Jefferson Barracks to be imprisoned down in St. Louis. He was placed in shackles and put on a raft with Jefferson. Just north of here, he begged Jefferson to unshackle him. It would shame him in front of the Mesquaukie tribe.

"Can you picture him down there in white? Jefferson agreed to unshackle him. That way, he could raise his hands above his head as he passed by this bluff and the village.

"You know, Mom, there is something very interesting that made me see him in a different light. When he was younger, he found two white boys who were either orphaned or cut off from their parents. Black Hawk brought them home, and he and his wife Singing Bird adopted them.

"That would drive Grandma crazy. She would be trying to locate all parents who lost two boys," Miki said, and then she laughed.

"Or to see if the parents had died. She'd want to solve the mystery of who those boys' parents were," said Noel.

"That's funny and so true," agreed Miki.

"You know what? I feel so much better. I'm ready to go home and sleep."

"I'm glad you came with us, no sense suffering alone at home," said Franklin kindly.

"Me, too. Mom."

Franklin took a couple more pictures of the Mississippi. "Let me get another picture of the two of you looking down at the river."

"I want to write my book. I'm free from caregiving forever," said Noel with relief.

Chapter Thirty-Nine

ON THE WAY BACK to Noel's house, she received a phone call.

"Hi, Mom. What's going on?"

Miki noticed as the color drained from her mother's face. She pulled the car to the side of the road and stopped. She and Franklin sat quietly while Noel finished the phone call.

Noel clicked end on her phone.

"What's up, Mom?"

"Grandma received a letter. She said she didn't recognize the name on the return address."

"You're scaring me now, what is it?"

"There's a girl from Dubuque who says she was adopted. She was looking at her mother's paperwork from the adoption, and she saw a name written in pencil on the other side of the paper. It was Mom's name."

"How is that possible?"

"I'm not sure, but she told Grandma she's been looking for her baby sister for forty-three years."

"Does she think she's your sister?" asked Miki.

"I think she does. She's in Dubuque. She lives near the monastery now outside of town. Mom gave me her number.

"I asked her about my birth mother, but Mom didn't want to tell me on the phone. She did say her name is Adriana Bishop." She paused and said quietly, "Adriana…Bishop? Adriana…Bishop. So, my real name is Bishop."

Chapter Forty

Noel drove out on Highway 151 alone and turned onto Monastery Road.

"I'm lost, there are so many new subdivisions out here."

Finally, she found the address.

Wasn't the day emotional enough without something like this?

She was shaking and felt sick to her stomach, so she sat in the car for several minutes before she finally got out and walked up the sidewalk.

The front door opened, and Noel stopped.

Noel's eyes locked with the woman. It surprised her how much they looked alike.

Noel's legs started to give out.

"No, don't fall!" The woman hurried out to Noel, grabbed her arm, and they walked into the house together.

They sat on the sofa, and the woman said, "You're my sister. All this time I wondered what happened to you. But I believed you were near." She put her arm around Noel and hugged her, and Noel hugged back as though she might lose her again if she let go.

"What's your name? Are you married? Do you have kids?" Noel asked the questions so fast her sister didn't get a chance to answer the first one, and they both laughed.

"Mary Kaye with an e, and yes, I'm married. My husband's name is Matt, and we have four grown kids."

"Are *you* married?"

"I will be. I just saw my ex-husband, and we're thinking of getting back together, we don't have a date yet." She waved her hand in front of her. "But that's another story." She smiled. "I have one daughter."

The two ladies laughed and then burst into tears." I'm so glad I found you," said Mary Kaye.

"Me, too," said Noel. "So, what happened to our parents?"

"Dad was in the Navy when they met. After you were born, we lived happily for two and a half years. Dad was out to sea for at least eighteen months of that, I think. Mom was diagnosed with terminal cancer right after he shipped off, and she had no way to contact him."

"That's awful."

"Dad had just left, Mom wanted us to be together. But no one would take both of us, and she was getting sicker and in so much pain. So, they accepted an offer in another county. Mom kept me another month while they searched for a family for me. I was twelve, no one wanted an older girl.

"Then a miracle happened. An older couple heard about our situation. They came to see me, and soon I packed my clothes. Mom made a special dress for me before she got sick. It was lavender with a broad white collar with lace on the edge. I was wearing it when they picked me up. I remember I was sitting on the edge of mother's bed, and she pushed my bangs out of my face.

"She told me she should have cut my hair and wondered what my new parents would think of her. She gave me her hope chest and my sewing machine.

"I told her thanks for teaching me to sew, that's the one thing I remember the most. She told me, 'Whenever you sew on that machine, I'll be there right next to you.'

"I told Mom I didn't want to leave her because she needed me. She so wanted you and I to know each other. She said she wouldn't give you up without knowing where you were. Mom didn't want you to become a ward of the state, she wanted you adopted and know who would adopt you."

Mary Kaye showed Noel a newspaper. "I found this article in the paper about it. Look at the back. This name, Antoinette Holmes, Clayton Co was in pencil, and the handwriting looked shaky. I guess someone did tell Mom who adopted you, or at least tried to."

"Was our dad in your life?"

"Yes, when he came back, I lived here with him on the weekends. It was an open adoption. The couple I was with had health problems. I was able to get an emancipation from them and live with Dad full time at sixteen. I joined the band in the fourth grade. He came to all the football games and watched me in the parades. Dad took me over every weekend, and we helped Barbara and Dean, the older couple who adopted me."

"Does Dad live here?"

"Yes. He's still in the little house we lived in. He never wanted to leave where his family was. He never stopped thinking of you."

"I would like to meet him."

"Yes. Our house was one of the first houses here before all the subdivisions."

The two cried again.

"We'll never be apart again. I'll look out for you," said Mary Kaye. "I still have some of the dresses mother made. C'mon, I'll show you."

They held the dresses in front of themselves admiring them in the mirror.

"They are so cute. She also made this winter coat. I wear it some-times.

"Mom said she would always be there when I was sewing, and I feel she is here with us now. She's happy you are seeing her things."

Noel was barely listening. She held a dress close to her face, drink-ing in the smell of her mother. She never wanted to let go of it.

"May I keep this?" asked Noel.

"Sure."

"That's what Mom would want. I'm just so happy."

"Thank you." Noel draped the dress over her arm.

"Is it possible to go see our dad?"

"Yes, he'll be so thrilled. I'll drive and bring along some photos."

Several minutes later, they were standing at their father's door.

Mary Kaye rang the doorbell. "His name is Andrew."

"Mary Kaye! Good to see you, c'mon in."

"Daddy, I have someone special for you to meet. I found her, Daddy, this is Noel."

"Wait? My real name is Noel? I've always been Noel? Wow! So, my mom, Nettie, kept my original name."

"May I give you a hug?" asked Andrew.

Noel smiled, and they hugged briefly.

"You can call me Andy or Dad, whatever you are comfortable with. It was so hard to lose you and your mother. I wasn't even there to say good-bye to you, and it broke my heart. You were always a daddy's girl."

"I was? I didn't know that."

"I can't believe this is happening. You were suffering all this time. Dad and I were right here in Dubuque for the last twenty-four years."

"Is that right? My goodness. If I only knew."

"Finding you changes everything. I was thinking about moving to Elkton to help my mom, but no way now. I didn't have a dad. I was adopted by a single woman."

"Was she good to you?'

"She's a wonderful mother. Her name is Antoinette Holmes, you'll like her. She's a genealogist and has tried to help me find you."

"She's all right with you having us in your life?"

"Oh, yes. She fully supports it." Noel assured her dad.

"Mom loved Christmas. She loved to decorate," said Mary Kaye.

"She did? I like decorating for Christmas, too. I can't wait till you see my mother's Christmas villages. They're amazing." Noel's eyes sparkled.

"Our mom made us all kinds of holiday outfits," said Mary Kaye. "She made this cute little black and orange witch dress for you. I saved it, although, I let my daughter wear it. It's in the hope chest."

Andrew studied Noel. "After all these years, you're really here.

"The last time I saw you, I threw you in the air right over there in front of the door. You laughed and laughed, and I thought in six months you will be so different. I wanted to memorize how you looked. Then we walked outside, and I got in the car. You did the cutest thing. You laid in the grass in the front yard on your tummy. Then you propped yourself up on your elbows and put your hands on your cheeks. You posed with the most darling smile, and I reached in the car and grabbed my camera and took your picture. Then I hugged your mother and got in the car. I couldn't look back, or I would never leave. I never dreamed that I would never see you again."

Tears gathered in the corners of his eyes. He pulled out his wallet, retrieved the picture, and showed it to the two women. "I had it above my bunk in the ship."

"I'm so sorry, Dad. How you suffered, too."

"But you're here now."

"And I have pictures, too, of me growing up." She opened her wallet. "Here's Mom, I'm so blessed to have her."

"I'm glad you had her, too."

The three whiled away the afternoon looking at pictures and reminiscing about their lives. It got very late, and Mary Kaye asked, "Do you want to stay the night, Noel?"

"That might be nice."

The excitement of the day was over. All her mysteries were revealed, and now Noel did not feel happy. She felt anxious.

She thought about Nettie in Elkton, staring at the ceiling thinking about what she had said to her earlier today. That she doesn't care if she ever went back to Elkton. She felt bad, knowing that must have been hard for her mom to hear.

Noel was tired. She decided she shouldn't think anymore. But now she knew, after forty-two years, she had been loved in two places.

Throughout the fall, Noel stayed at home with her biological family. She decided it was time for her to write her book. Every day, she stuck with her new habit of writing from five a.m. till ten. Plus, doing research about all the countries Albert had visited in 1909. She identified pictures and learned the backstory to endless subjects. She poured all her ideas onto the page.

Then she made many plans with her sister and nieces. Nettie was always excited to get her calls to keep her abreast of her writing. The rest of the time she spent dating Hank all over again. And she rediscovered all the things she once loved about him, except, it was all much better this time. They even went to marriage counseling.

Chapter Forty-One

NETTIE SMILED mischievously at her granddaughter. "It's St. Nicolas Day tomorrow. You better be good, or you'll get coal in your stocking in the morning."

Miki put her hands on her hips. "Is that a real thing?"

"Yes, but getting a chunk of coal in your stocking back then was a wonderful gift. Poor people were freezing, and you would be so grateful to have some coal to burn. I guess when people stopped using coal, it became a negative."

"Speaking of people who should get coal. Those two old biddies Anita Bath and Fanny Sniff came by the museum. One wanted to make sure we weren't selling any antiques there. Then they saw books about American history and thought we were selling them. I told her they were donated, and we give them away as prizes. They are always so negative." Miki shook her head.

"Yea, it makes you wonder. Sometimes, I want to criticize them, but I can't help but wonder what they're childhoods were like to make such characters. Perhaps they never were given gifts in their lives. Maybe that's why they are so sour."

"Maybe, but still, they are adults now—time to grow up."

"I'm going to give them each a gift," said Nettie. "Maybe they would like a church, what do you think?"

"I think that's a great idea, Grandma."

Miki helped Nettie wrap them in bright red foil Christmas wrap finished with a bow, ribbon, and a card.

Nettie wrote a card addressed to each of them.

It occurred to me that you may not get many gifts. I hope this will be to your liking. Happy St. Nicholas Day. Sincerely,

Your Friend, Nettie.

Pleased with her idea, she thought she might reach their cold, critical hearts. First, she went to the bookstore and gave Anita her gift.

"This is so sweet of you, all the hard work you put into your valuable art." Anita opened the box and lifted it out. "Nettie, this is beautiful!"

She plugged it in. "Look how beautiful," she said to her customers.

"I will always cherish this, Nettie. My dad abandoned us when I was little, and our mother never had money for gifts. Thank you. This is a Happy St. Nicholas Day."

"I'm so happy. Merry Christmas, Anita."

"Same to you Ms. Holmes, and thank you."

Nettie's heart was happy when she walked into Miss Fanny's antique store and repeated the entire scene with much the same reaction.

A few days later, Nettie went shopping. As she walked along Main Street, she passed by the antique store, and her heart warmed when she saw her church in the window. It was for sale and bore a ninety-nine-dollar price tag. At first, she was hurt, but then she realized someone would buy it and enjoy it, and that would be wonderful.

Further down the street, she stopped in the bookstore on her way home. Anita approached Nettie the minute she walked in. "Did you see my display?"

Anita grabbed Nettie's arm and dragged her to a special table near the reading chairs. There was the church sitting at the top of the display among white batting and surrounded by figurines, trees, and animals.

"Everyone can enjoy your gift now, Nettie. I get so many compliments."

"It exudes Christmas joy, doesn't it."

"Yes, it does." Anita's satisfied look made Nettie smile. She noticed a book in Nettie's had. "Take that book, Nettie. It's my gift to you. Merry Christmas."

"Thank you, Anita. Merry Christmas."

Chapter Forty-Two

DECEMBER 5, 2008, The Barn Community Center on Main Street was bursting with excitement as the center of the Volunteer Christmas Party for Main Street Alive!

Wonderful smells of ham, scalloped potatoes, pumpkin pie, and cinnamon apple cider welcomed guests the minute they stepped through the door.

A variety of Christmas trees with colored lights and construction paper garland and ornaments made by the elementary school children garnished the stage and surrounded the dance floor.

The mayor stepped to the podium. "Friends, this is why I love this town!" The guests burst into applause.

A mother and child tried to get the mayor's attention. He bent down to their level, and the woman spoke quietly to Mayor Frommelt, and he held the mic for the little girl.

"My sister and I made this for you."

"Oh, how festive. Thank you, can you tell us your name?"

"Navy, my sister is Jemma."

"How old are you?"

"I'm fouwa."

"Well, Jemma and Navy, thank you so much. May I shake your hands?"

They each smiled and shook his hand as a volunteer snapped a picture. An assistant pinned the boutonniere on the mayor's jacket.

Mayor Frommelt stepped back to the podium. "As I was saying, I *love* this town. So many pulling together, volunteering your time and talents to help improve our *big* little town. We're big in spirit and caring, and I thank you. I'm sure we will see our town become even bigger with our Main Street Alive! project completed. Thank you again, and enjoy your dinner and dance, you earned it."

Christmas music started softly creating a festive ambiance, and laughter melted into the feel of Christmas. The youth served plates of food and pitchers of cider.

North came through the door, and Nettie waved him over to their table. "Where's your dad?"

"He sent Granny and Grandma ahead with me. She had a leak under the kitchen sink."

"Oh, no, that's too bad."

"You should know Dad reads and studies all the stories you gave to us," said North. "He can't stop studying it either. It's all because of you. He finds them fascinating, and he can't wait to meet you in person."

"Thank you for telling me that, North. I can't wait to meet him. He's a wonderful father, I can see that in you. Did you see the sheriff's gift to the museum?"

"No." He shook his head.

"It's his great-grandfather's Holland sleigh. It was left in his dad's barn before they tore it down. Now it's right in the front window of the museum, and I love it."

"I'll have to see it."

"I can't wait to see the work you did on the baby Jesus. Only two and one-half weeks till Christmas Eve."

"It looks great, all that's left is the gold trim. You would never guess the arms were ever broken off. The old Elkport Nativity will travel to Elkton for this year and then back to Elkport."

The DJ cranked up a fun Benny Goodman song "Sing, Sing, Sing." It filled the room, and all the old folks converged on the dance floor.

Nettie started dancing a modified Charleston, and Miki, Franklin, and the mayor joined in.

"Can you do the Charleston?" asked Franklin.

"If memory serves." Miki stepped in front of Franklin.

They started with the Bee's Knees, making a circle separately with jazz hands, then they traveled across the floor. He grasped her shoulders, sliding her legs between his feet, and then quickly snapped her up. He twirled her around his waist to the clapping and cheering of the guests.

Suddenly, Nettie felt a little light-headed and lost her balance. The mayor and Franklin helped her to a chair and put her feet up.

"Are you okay, Grandma?" Miki knelt next to Nettie.

The DJ changed direction and started the raffle drawing.

"I'm fine. I'm not sure what happened."

Franklin carried her to the back of the room.

"It's okay, just relax, Mom," said Noel

North stepped into the room. "Want some punch, Nettie?"

She took the paper cup. "Thank you. I seem to be very thirsty. I think I'll need another, North."

"Dad just got here. I'll get you another drink."

Nettie took the last sip of punch and looked up to see North with a man she assumed was his dad.

North handed Nettie another cup of punch. "Nettie, this is my dad, Nicolas Keller."

Nicolas stepped forward with a big smile.

Startled, Nettie stood quickly and studied his face, the empty cup dropped out of her hand. Her mind whirled with a flashback to dancing with a smiling Caleb at a barn dance. Looking at Nicolas, she could only see Caleb.

"You…you're *you*, my…son."

Nicolas recoiled. "What?"

Nettie's eyes rolled back in her head, and she passed out.

Granny Keller and Bernice were standing nearby, both stunned to see Nettie faint. Bernice dropped the box of beads she was holding, and Granny dropped her purse.

Nicolas said, "Let's get Nettie on the couch, North."

Suzie poked her head in. "Should I call 911?"

"Yes," North and Nicolas chorused.

"I'll get smelling salts from the office," said the mayor. He returned shortly with the first aid kit and waved the smelling salts under Nettie's nose.

Nettie opened her eyes to Doc Warner holding a stethoscope on her chest. She abruptly sat up and pushed it away. "Forget about this, my health is not the problem."

Granny snapped at Beatrice. "Now look what's happened! I told you right from the start this was a bad idea."

Beatrice began to hyperventilate, and she hurried from the room. Granny followed her and started to help Bernice with her coat, but then threw her hat and scarf at her, and walked out the door, with Bernice right behind her.

Outside, Granny couldn't hold in her feelings anymore. "You have no one to blame but yourself. We need to give him the box right now. I sensed something about her that day at the blacksmith shop. She's Nick's birth mother, I'm sure of it."

Beatrice fell to her knees on the sidewalk, sobbing. People on the street asked if she needed any help, but she just cried.

Granny picked up the keys from the sidewalk and walked down to the car.

Beatrice grabbed onto a parking meter and pulled herself up. She was still crying when she got to the car.

"Now, now. It's not the end of the world." Granny tried to comfort her. "You and my son have a whole new family all at once. You have a right to be overwhelmed. Take my arm, Little Bea. No matter what you do, you will always be my Little Bea. My stubborn little Beatrice."

"What do you think is going on in there right now?" asked Beatrice.

"Well, that's not our concern. Let's go home and get his birth box and do the right thing."

The doctor said, "No more of this now. Let's get you checked out. Get her into the ambulance," he said to the two EMT's.

"I don't know what she's talking about, Dad, the son thing."

"I hope you're all right, Nettie."

An EMT put an oxygen mask over Nettie's face, and Noel climbed in the front while they loaded her into the ambulance.

"I wonder if she's getting dementia or maybe a stroke?" ventured North.

Nicolas shrugged. "I don't know." He watched the ambulance drive away. "I'm going home and talk to my mother…if she is my mother."

Chapter Forty-Three

When Nicolas Keller arrived home, his dad was standing in the doorway. "What's going on, Dad?"

Mom looked down.

"Mom, is this Nettie person my real mother?"

Dad shook his head. "I don't know for sure, Nick, but she believes she is."

"What? Aren't you my parents?" Tears welled up in his eyes.

"Of course, we are!" Mom blurted.

Dad looked at his wife and slowly shook his head. "We are not your biological parents, Nick."

His mom bolted from the room, sobbing.

"Dad! How can you do that to me after all these years. How will I ever trust you again? I'm so angry at both of you!"

He pushed past his father and into the kitchen where his mother was crying unconsolably. She looked at her son with blood shot eyes and wiped her nose.

"So, what do you have to say for yourself, Mom?" Nick was not letting his parents off the hook.

His dad came into the kitchen. "I didn't want to keep this a secret, son, but Bea felt it was best."

Bea's voice broke. "I was afraid I would lose you, and I didn't want someone else taking you from me."

"I'm forty-five. I'm not a child. All those years I wondered why I was so different from my brothers. One time, I even said to myself I feel like I must have been adopted. We have nothing in common, except we lived on this farm. I feel so betrayed! I don't even know who *I am* anymore."

Nicolas stormed out of the room.

Minutes later, he stormed out the front door. "I have no idea when I'll be back." He slammed his truck into gear, lost in a turmoil of thought, he sped out of the driveway.

North knocked briefly on Granny Keller's door before walking in.

Grandma was sitting near the fireplace.

"So, Grandma, is this why you were so cold to Nettie that day she came over? You were rude, and I was embarrassed. She's my friend. She was doing *your* genealogy."

"I didn't want her snooping around in our life."

"Because she would find out your little secret?"

"I didn't know she was his mother North, we still don't. She might be deranged."

"Dad is so upset. I've never seen him this way before," cried North.

"I wanted to tell him," said his grandfather. "But Bea was afraid this other woman would make trouble and turn him against us. Since that's what she wanted, I backed her up because she's my wife, but I knew that it was a bad idea."

North sighed. "Well, I'm going to the hospital to check on my friend. No matter who she is."

My dad is *adopted. Is Nettie my grandmother? What about Miki, is she, my cousin? I was interested in her. Nettie wanted me to be.*

Chapter Forty-Four

NICK DROVE AROUND for two hours ending up in a cornfield, parked, and cried till there were no more tears.

I knew something was wrong so many times growing up. "I can't believe this." Nick got out of the truck, collapsed on the ground, and screamed, "God, wasn't it bad enough my wife had to die? Do you hate me? I've tried so hard to be good."

Overcome with cold, he climbed back in his truck and drove back to town. He thought of going home to face his mother.

I can't stand going back there. I don't want to argue with her. I know she raised me; I just can't stand it.

The angrier he got, the faster he drove. The sun warmed that day and melted some of the snow, and now it is well below zero. He was going too fast for town. "I better slow down, what am I doing?"

Something darted in front of him, and he slammed on the brakes, causing the truck to fishtail out of control. He heard a pitiful yelp as the truck launched over a ditch and through a fence landing in the pastor's front yard.

The porch light came on, and the pastor ran out of the house.

Nick was shaken and had a huge bump on his head but seemed to be okay.

The pastor and his wife brought Nick into their house where he sat close to their fire, while Nick poured his heart out.

The pastor said, "I remember when your wife died, what a tragedy. Losing the love of your life and the mother of your child is one of the hardest losses to face, but I wonder if you might be over stressing a little about this. I know you feel betrayed, and you have a right to feel anger and hurt. But no one is dead, right? I can tell you this, I have known Nettie for years, and you have nothing to fear from her. I had no idea that she had a son or whether she is correct, but I don't think this situation is as bad as you think it is."

Mrs. Haynes asked, "Your parents were good to you, right?"

"Yes."

"Exactly, they adopted you, loved you, and they didn't treat you any different than their biological children."

Nick nodded. "No. That's true."

"And if it's true, and Nettie has a nice family, would it be bad to have more family?"

"If Nettie is my mother, that means that she loved me enough to have me, and then she had to give me up."

The pastor's wife rocked in her chair. "That must have been very hard. How old are you?"

"Forty-five," answered Nick.

"That would mean she waited forty-five years to find you. That's a long time," reasoned Mrs. Haynes.

"Yeah, I guess I didn't think about it like that."

"Well, you were in shock, son. Perfectly normal," said Pastor Haynes.

"Why don't we all go over to the hospital and see how Nettie is doing. I want to give her a blessing."

Nick stood. "Okay. Wait, I think I hit a dog."

"What dog?" Mrs. Haynes stopped rocking.

"Just after I slammed on the brakes, a dog ran out in front of my truck. I heard it yelp, so I'm pretty sure I hit it."

Pastor Haynes grabbed a flashlight, and the two men ran into the street. The pastor shined his flashlight in every direction, but no dog, and no pawprints in the snow.

"Are you sure you hit something?"

"I don't understand it." Nick rubbed his hands through his hair.

"I know what I saw. There must be internal bleeding."

Pastor Haynes' wife backed out of the garage, the pastor got in the car, and Nick followed them to the hospital.

When they arrived, Nick was surprised to see his son's truck in the parking lot. They located Nettie's room and found Noel and Miki sitting on either side of Nettie's bed. Nettie was asleep.

Peter Keller and Granny approached Nettie's bed. Granny carried an old dress box.

They waited for Nettie to wake, and then Granny handed her the box. "This belongs to you, Nettie."

Tears ran down Peter's face. "Nettie, was your son born on March 15, 1958?"

She nodded.

Peter touched her hand. "I want you to know, Ms. Nettie, I did not want to keep his adoption a secret, but my wife did. I'm sorry that you didn't get to spend time with him. I want you to know I appreciate your sacrifice, and we loved him so much. I'm so grateful to you. I don't know if you realized that he has the middle name you chose. I told my wife that I wanted Emanuel to be his middle name because that was our way of honoring your sacrifice."

Tears spilled down Nettie's cheeks, but she said nothing.

Miki covered her mouth with her hand and looked at Noel.

The birthday cake was for her son.

"That was the secret?" Noel looked down. "Mom, I'm sorry."

A nurse came into the room and asked them all to step out for a few minutes.

"May I have a few minutes?" asked Pastor Haynes.

"Okay, I'll be right back then."

The pastor anointed Nettie's head with oil and prayed for her health.

"Thank you, Pastor Haynes."

North and his dad came back into the room, but Nicolas hung back.

North stepped up to her bed. "I'll pray for you to get well, Nettie. I love you." He walked past his dad. "I'll leave you two alone, Dad."

Nicolas motioned to the box and sat in a nearby chair. "What is this?"

"Some things we made for you. I gave it to the adoption agency, so you could know about us." She paused. "You look just like your father."

"Do I?" Nicolas nodded briefly. "You should rest—maybe you could tell me about when I was born, and about my biological father tomorrow."

"Tell North I said to give you my Roi-Tan box tomorrow. I'll tell you a little about him."

"Is he alive?" asked Nicolas.

"No. He died before you were born," she barely whispered.

"Ummm. Okay, tomorrow is another day. Call me tomorrow—here's my number." He touched her hand. "Goodnight, Nettie."

"Goodnight, Nicolas." She closed her eyes.

❧

Nicolas glanced back before he left the room.

He stepped out into the night and looked up at the moon. *What a crazy night this has been. Two hours ago, I was a raging maniac, and now I've met a woman I never met before today, who claims to be my mother. And none of it would have happened if it weren't for that dog. I did see it, and I know I hit it. Maybe the dog was my Christmas miracle.*

On the way home, Nick stopped at the accident site. He got out of his truck and walked around. A little way from where he went in the ditch, he did find some paw prints in the snow. He stood still, running the accident over in his mind.

He suddenly spun around, feeling as though someone was looking at him. It was the dog. A collie-shepherd mix with black markings on its face.

The dog just stared at him.

"Come here, boy." Nick squatted. "Come here. I want to thank you."

The dog slowly came toward him. Its tail wagging. He barked when he reached Nicolas.

"Are you hurt, baby?" The dog moved closer, and Nick patted its head. He looked at the collar.

TAMMY.

"You're a girl. C'mon, I'll look out for you."

Nick started the truck, let the dog in the passenger side, and drove home. Just as he turned in the driveway, he said, "I can't wait to get into bed, I'm…Tammy? Where are you?"

He looked in the back seat. Nothing. He put his face in his hands.

"I need sleep."

Chapter Forty-Five

The next day, the doctor advised Nettie that her heart had weakened and he gave her instructions to go home, but she would need to rest.

North brought the Roi-Tan box with him when he and his dad picked up Nettie. The three drove down to Elkport together.

She told them the story about growing up in Elkport, about the sleigh ride, and growing up with Nicolas' father. She showed them the pictures of them in front of the church and Caleb's high school graduation photo.

Nicolas looked at the graduation picture. "I do look just like him. We don't need a DNA test, do we?"

"It's up to you, a mere formality."

Nettie told them about how Caleb died and about the ring.

Nicolas was stunned. "North gave the ring to Miki, without knowing the significance? It must have killed you to see him give it to Miki."

Nettie shrugged. "Well, he didn't know, and I never saw the ring because he never did give it to me, so I didn't have any attachment. I assumed it was lost forever."

Nettie touched the treasure box she made for her son. "Caleb was shocked a week earlier when I told him I was pregnant. He was so handsome and all the Bible reading in the world wasn't enough to keep me from his embrace. We looked into each other's eyes and knew we were meant to be. It was just one night, but our lives were changed forever.

"Caleb told his father about the situation, and the two men decided we must marry right away. His father and mother said that I was a good choice since they knew my family. It was decided by Caleb's parents that we could have an heirloom, their great-grand-mother's wedding solitaire.

"His parents brought out the jewelry box. His father told him that they took the diamond out of the solitaire for his mother's wedding ring and replaced it with a semi-precious sapphire. They told him if he didn't mind the sapphire, he could have it for a wedding ring.

"He knew I would love it and said he imagined me wearing it.

"We were to marry the next Saturday at church. I would make an appropriate dress for the occasion, and we would marry with just our families attending.

"The day before the flood, he took me over to the church to show me the completed Nativity. It was beautiful. He said our situation was his fault, and for me not to feel guilty. He promised he would work hard and make it up to me, and that our baby would be the most special boy or girl in the world, wanted and loved by us.

"Then, after Caleb's funeral, my mother and I drove to the family cemetery, and she counseled me not to take on this responsibility of a child alone.

"I wasn't sure what she was talking about. She asked me if I loved my baby, and, of course, I said I did. She said, don't you think he deserves a mother and a father, and that a boy needs a father. She said, boys grow up, they don't stay little, and unfortunately, my father wasn't in the best of health. She was concerned that my dad may not last until Emmanuel was grown, and how would I do it by myself.

"I told my mother that I didn't think she had the right to tell me whether I should love my baby or give him to someone else. I told her she was insensitive.

"Two months later, my mother took me to the cemetery where I put some prairie flowers on Caleb's grave. I blew him a kiss and promised I would take good care of our child. We got in my parents' 1948 Plymouth and headed to the train station. I was to spend the next five and a half months up in Minnesota with my aunt and her husband. The next spring, I realized that my mother was probably right. I felt like I already disappointed her once, and I didn't want to do it twice.

"My baby deserved the best, and that wasn't me, not at this time. So, after I returned home, my mother drove me to the adoption agency. Every step was a step closer to leaving my boy forever. The worker approached me with a heavy caring smile. My heart was on the floor. This was so unreal, I couldn't believe it was happening. She slowly reached out for my Emmanuel, and I gave him to her, but my heart didn't.

"I gave her the dress box. Inside was a quilt that I made for him while I was pregnant. Multicolored, because I didn't know if it would be a boy or girl. It had perfect little pastel squares of flannel, soft for his touch. I put in a rattle and a toy train his granddad had whittled out of wood for him. My mother knitted him a cap and booties. And lastly, a picture of his mother and father together in front of the church holding hands at sixteen and eighteen."

"Oh my gosh, the baby," said Nicolas. "Jesus from the Nativity is in his one arm and you in the other. You looked so pretty."

Nettie breathed deeply, motioning to the picture. "The set used to be just varnished. Caleb was the first one to paint it, making them come to life."

"I think I know how he would have felt. I did the carving, too, of the arms that broke off using woodworking and carving skills."

"He was a deep thinker when it came to his relationship with God." Nettie smiled at Nicolas.

He said, "I saw his name painted on the bottom. I had no idea it was my own father. How can a person deny that it was destiny. We loved the same things. He had this with him when he died, it may have helped him stay above water for a while. It gives me goose-bumps. I can't bring him back to life, but I can fix this physical symbol of the Savior to inspire the people at church, just the way he did. I wish I could have had a lesson with my father to understand how he mixed the paint colors. I'll do my best to match the baby's arms to the rest of the carving."

Nicolas' eyes brightened. "Now I understand where my inspiration for art comes from. I've always wondered about that."

"He would have loved you as powerfully as you feel about him now. He had that caring respectful side," said Nettie.

"I understand why you never married. When you find your exact Soulmate, how do you find that twice? Especially, when you grow up together."

Nettie covered his hand with hers, and mother and son sat silently in each other's presence, absorbing the power of being together, finally.

Nicolas lifted the quilt out of the box.

"You were wrapped in it when I gave you to them."

"Yes, in this picture," said Nicolas, "I am wrapped in it.".

"I made copies for myself, so I could remember what you looked like. I wanted you to know that I kept you for a month and held you and snuggled with you. Your little eyes trying to fix a gaze from the sound of my voice. You were so intent on seeing me.

"Now, you were being whisked away, but I told myself this is only temporary, that I would see you someday as an adult. I knew I had signed a paper waiving my rights, but I was standing at the edge of darkness. The feelings of doom tried to pull me down into the pit. There is no hope there. It's ghastly. I cried until there was nothing left to feel.

"I walked out the door and down the steps feeling the full weight of being an adult. That there are consequences to all our actions. I went to my bedroom, locked my door, pulled the shade, and sat in the dark. The morning sun rose, the rooster crowed, but my room never was light. After three days, my hunger drove me to open the door and acknowledge there was a whole world out there that is untouched by my sad thoughts.

"My mother brought me a tray with a bowl of oatmeal, the melted brown sugar, a pat of butter pressed in the center, cream from our Jersey cows around the edges. It reminded me of my childhood when mother prepared breakfast each day for us kids after milking, before the school bus arrived.

"Along with the oatmeal was a serving of comfort, a mother's love in the form of a flower from her garden. Her love for me had changed. From then on out, she always talked to me like an adult. I miss my mama.

"With time, I imagined he would see my treasure box for him. Not seeing him is what I deserve. It's my punishment.

"Our home is gone now. This was our yard." Nettie turned to the left. "This is where Papa and I buried Glory, under the arched oak tree in the front yard. Over under that tree is my dog Tammy. Papa had told me I was so sad, but that these trees would grow to be tall. That was so Glory and Tammy could look out for me. One tree a mighty oak and the other a cottonwood. It was all so symbolic."

"Wait, you said Tammy was your dog? What did she look like?"

"She was a mutt, a collie-shepherd mix with a pretty freckled face."

Nicolas said, "I know this will sound crazy, but I saw that dog."

"Impossible, she's been dead forty years."

"No, I did. The night I came to the hospital with Pastor Haynes. She was wearing a leather collar with her name engraved on brass."

Nettie was surprised. "That was her collar. I kept it."

"She ran out in front of me at the pastor's house. And then he came out, and he and his wife talked to me about this whole situation. That's why I'm able to talk to you about this now."

"Well, she saved both of us, didn't she?"

"I put her in my truck and drove to my parents' house, but she literally disappeared."

Nettie grabbed his hand. "It was really her, Nicolas. Thank you, Tammy, you brought me together with my son."

Chapter Forty-Six

NETTIE HANDED Nick the Roi-Tan box. He stared at her. "I can't believe you are my biological mother. I feel like I should have known it."

"What about me? I had no idea, either. It's just perfect though, isn't it?"

Nick smiled and nodded.

"How will I deal with my mother? I don't even feel like she is my mother. She made my life a lie."

"I understand it was a shock. I've found you now, and I don't care anymore. Life is short, we just need to forgive and move on. I'm happy to spend as much time with you as I can this Christmas."

Over the next two and a half weeks, Nick made copious notes of all the things Nettie could tell him about her life and her relatives. He dropped by to bring her a meal or some flowers. North did the same thing. She seemed to be on the mend, and all of them were excited to share their lives together. One time, they drove under the arches downtown enjoying the new signage, and Nettie gave them a tour of the museum and the new garret and windmill.

<h1 style="text-align:center">Chapter Forty-Seven</h1>

CHRISTMAS EVE all the family gathered for dinner at Nettie's. The house was decked out with more lights than ever. Noel and her sister Mary Kaye happily added to what Miki and Nettie had already done.

Nettie and Miki had never seen Noel this way before. She seemed to love Christmas now and seemed to be more at peace with herself.

Hank and Miki learned to feel at home with their new family. Andy was also there, and, of course, Nicolas and North.

Linny, as Miki now called him, had arrived two days ago.

The guests were all impressed by Nettie's Victorian houses and streets, and how beautifully the table was set. A turkey in the oven filled the house with a salivating aroma. So many luscious smells.

Miki was spinning the vinyl with the most discriminating taste. They turned off the overhead lights, and guests enjoyed looking at all the displays.

Nettie led a tour of her grandma's house like she was at the museum.

"Grandma calls this Church Street because there are so many beautiful churches." She pointed to another part. "Over there is the bad side of town. Taverns, grog shops, and a beer factory with the train running in front of it."

Nettie pushed a button, and a realistic train whistle blew, and a ticket man yelled, "All aboard!" Steam released, and the wheels began clickety-clacking down the track.

A little porcelain man with a loaded dolly was leaving the train station, Victorian clad passengers each had a piece of luggage.

Miki observed with childhood joy. She pointed out the school yard filled with children involved in various childhood activities accustomed to children in the 1800's. A seesaw, a boy with a ring and a stick, a brown dog in tow. Children making a snowman. A boy on a bench reading a book.

Nettie turned on all the battery-operated lights. A green reindeer with a red nose on top of a bookstore, a blinking bare, ball-shaped tree, and a dress shop with a Victorian lady gaily costumed in red and green.

"I call her the Christmas Lady," said Nettie with pride. "Isn't she fancy?" She pointed out a candle shop with an evergreen in front, and a policeman leaning forward talking to a little girl with a wrapped gift box behind his back.

A toy store filled with a toy train, a dolly, a doll house, and a sled. A detailed watch shop with real display windows. People out of dimension with the houses were looking in the second story windows.

Behind them was a man climbing a ladder to light the old-fashioned gas lamp on the street corner. The street sign said State and Main. A movie theater with colored lights around the word "Theater" vertically aligned. Multicolored lights around the outside of the buildings magnified the interesting architecture of each piece.

Lights had been carefully taped into place. Next were torn pieces of batting edged in, around, and under each building and over each lightbulb to hide the wires. Once the faux snowbanks were in place, tiny snowmen were displayed. Sleigh passengers in Victorian costume strategically placed on the hills.

The village was meant to represent the past; to make the older folks feel young again, and to remember how it used to be in their own neighborhoods.

Each piece was a treasure to Nettie.

Franklin studied the soft glow of a Victorian Christmas. He moved from display to display, studying each piece in detail.

"You must feel like these people are alive living in your frozen world," said Franklin with his face glowing from red and green blinking lights.

Nettie's display boasted a different street on every piece of furniture, including the North Pole on a curio case. Santa was perched on an ice throne with elves riding in trains, teaching reindeer to fly, and an adorable stable with all of Santa's deer inside, a name above each door. Dasher, Dancer, Prancer, Vixen, Comet, Cupid, Donner, and Blitzen.

"This street is special." Nettie pointed out to Miki and North. "The old-fashioned street sign, ENTERING CHRISTMASVILLE."

"I love the little man with a top hat and his woman. They are covered with a plaid blanket in a horse-drawn sleigh. It's neat the way they are entering a bridge, and the mirror under it looks just like a frozen lake. The way all the different colors are reflected in the clear ice blocks and off the lake. All the different types of trees here make it all seem so real." North was visibly impressed.

Miki said, "It takes a lot of love to make this. Weeks, huh, Grandma? I used to help you unbox all these. Thank heavens North helped us this year."

"Wouldn't you like to live here, North? In the village, I mean?" asked Nettie. "Life is what we make of it. We need a roof over our head and to be surrounded by the people we love. That's what I dream about when I look at my village."

Noel carried in a tray of hot chocolate with whipped cream, and they each took a mug.

"Did you put real whipping cream in this Noel?" asked Mary Kaye.

"Yes, no substitutes here. It's the Holmes way," Noel said with pride.

Nettie perked up. "Why don't we go to the dining room table, and everyone share your favorite Christmas memory?"

Linny seemed to feel at home here. North placed a lap quilt over

Miki's shoulders. She made eye contact with him and smiled.

North stated, "I saw the church you were making in the she-shed. It's at the end of the street in Christmasville."

Nettie had taped a large moon on the wall behind the steeple.

"Yes. It's the little town I grew up in." Nettie looked at Andy and Mary Kaye. "So many fond memories. I find that I want to remember more and more. It makes me feel good, I had a wonderful childhood."

Nettie glanced at Miki and then North. They seemed comfortable with each other.

Nettie pointed to a light grey building. "This was our house, Andy. My mama, Papa, and six kids, and of course, Tammy." She pointed to the running dog figurine chasing the sleigh. The dog's face had black accents that touched the edges of her pointy ears.

Nick jumped up to look at the little figurine. "That's the dog. It has the same happy look on its face."

"Caleb and I would hike all over the bluff behind the church with Tammy. One time, she spotted a rattler and warned us to stay away."

Nick looked at the dog again.

"Our favorite pastime was running up and down the bluffs under the tree canopies. The place seemed like heaven when you're a kid. Seasons roll by slowly when you are looking forward to being grown up. I remember hanging Christmas lights on the picket fence around the front yard. Something Caleb and I took over from Father when we were twelve."

"Your house was close to the bank?" asked Nicolas.

"Yes, it was, dear. We had a bank, a blacksmith shop, a general store, and, of course, the German Church right on this landing above the Turkey River. It's like a painting of a place that never really was. A figment of my imagination. Yet it seems like yesterday. Time is a funny thing."

"I'll say." Andy looked at Noel, and he reached for her hand.

Miki pointed to the special tree in front of her miniature lighted house.

"Is that the oak tree great-granddad planted in the front yard?" asked Miki.

"Yes. When Tammy passed, I was inconsolable. It was the first time I experienced death close to me. He said, 'Antoinette, lets you and I turn this sadness into a blessing.' He told me to grab a shovel, and we buried her in a sheet. He laid her respectfully in a deep grave, and then we planted an oak tree on top of her.

"My dad told me that way, this tree will grow tall, and she could always look over me. He was good at saying the right thing at just the right time. I miss that." A tear rolled down her cheek.

Nick listened intently to all these stories about the dog.

"Mom, what are you going to do with all this stuff?" asked Noel. "You could start giving it away, you'll never miss it."

Nettie didn't respond to her daughter.

North picked up a coffee table book, *Ghost Towns of Iowa*. He read the name of a town, "The Ghosts of Elkport." He spied a photo with a church on a rise. He held up a picture of the church next to the porcelain display.

"Nettie, you're recreating your childhood. Christmasville is Elkport." He smiled. "So, this is what Elkport used to look like?"

North passed the book around, so everyone could see Elkport in the old days. Hank gathered the empty cups of hot chocolate.

"That's really kind of you," said Noel.

"Well, useful." Miki teased.

"Let's bring on the turkey and the whole enchilada," said Lin.

"Where are you from, Mr. Enchilada?" asked Andy.

"San Francisco, but this is my home now."

"I lived in LA for eight years," said Andy.

Miki gave Franklin a surprised look.

Franklin said, "I left my heart in San Francisco—and here in Elkton."

Miki laughed. "Really, are you going to live here, too?"

"There's so much you don't know about me, dear." He took her hand, and they danced to the kitchen to get some food. When they came back into the room, Miki said, looking toward the window, "It's snowing!"

Evening came, and they all left to prepare for Christmas Eve service. They decided they would all return on Christmas Day to eat leftovers and play games together.

Nettie sat at the head of the table, alone. She thought about what Noel had said about giving away some of her things. She had been a little off put, but now she realized how much fun she could have wrapping her houses as gifts for the next day. She went to the back room to gather Christmas paper, tape, bows, and note cards.

She turned up the holiday music and unrolled the festive paper and ribbons. One by one, she took down the houses until she had one for each guest, plus two extras.

Feeling pleased with herself, she carefully placed them under the tree. Then, she went to her antique dresser to get something out of the top drawer. She took it back to the table and wrapped it.

She waited until time to leave for church. Then she called Nick to save her a place next to him and North. Nettie watched across the street for Suzie and her husband to leave with the kids. She then dropped off two packages on their front porch from her North Pole set, and followed directly behind.

She couldn't wait to walk in the snow.

It is so magical out there. The bare trees look like artwork.

Chapter Forty-Nine

ORTH TALKED to people who had come to view the restored Nativity before service.

He was asked, "Are you the young man who restored the set?"

"I just did the Jesus sculpture. My grandfather painted the whole set, and my father repaired the arms of the baby. I added the gold trim."

"It's beautifully painted. It brings so much meaning to this holy day," commented another.

He smiled humbly, thinking of the joy he was bringing to the congregation as Miss Sniff and Anita Bath approached the display.

"I hope the cost of this wasn't taken from the church budget," said Fanny.

"No, my dad and I volunteered. It's our gift to the congregation."

"Let's wish the pastor Merry Christmas before the service and get it over with," said Fanny. "I don't care for these late-night services."

Anita looked at her friend. "Sometimes, you're awfully negative. I think everything is beautiful." They walked away.

North approached Nicolas. "I just want you to know that I feel closer to you than I ever have. Merry Christmas." He hugged his dad.

Miki and Franklin examined the Nativity closer. While there, to Miki's surprise, Franklin bent down on one knee and asked her to marry him.

There was an audible shoosh and sigh in the front of the chapel when Franklin slipped the ring on her finger.

The pastor came out to start the service.

Hank with his arm around Noel, leaned forward to Miki. "I can't wait to have us all together again at Christmas dinner tomorrow."

Miki nodded. "We can't wait, either."

Noel held Hank's hand, and he looked at her like it was for the first time. "I've missed you. It's so good to be home again." Noel smiled and kissed his cheek.

Franklin wrapped his arm around Miki, and she held her hand up to show her father the ring.

"He just proposed at the creche before church."

"I heard."

Miki looked at Franklin. *You asked my dad?* And she loved him even more.

"I'm delighted." He kissed her fingers. He reached for Lin's hand and shook it. "We're all a family now," Hank said.

The pastor finished with his closing remarks, looked out on the congregation, and smiled.

"We had a German wood carver who made this Nativity set with so much care and love. We can only imagine how he felt to give such a gift to a congregation. This year, we get to enjoy this wonderful creche. This gift from an immigrant all those years ago to show his love and appreciation for his new home in a new land is much appreciated. Lift our hearts in celebration of the birth of a humble child and his parents. Let us sing as a closing hymn a song written by another young German in 1860, 'Stille Nacht, Heilige Nacht' or 'Silent Night, Holy Night.'"

Two guitarists stood and played an intro. The powerful organ joined in, everyone was filled with emotion.

Silent night. holy night, *Radiant beams from thy holy face.*
Son of God loves pure light. *With the dawn of redeeming grace*

A handful of snowflakes blew in the door behind the altar. The crystals were swept up high over the congregation where they bounced and played on the currents. The frosty friends were lifted and blown further up by the bellows of the organ and into the balcony.

Just then, a door opened to the belfry. Up higher still, they twinkled till they passed two bell ringers. Each boy took his turn to get pulled up wildly in the air. The one-of-a-kind crystals joined their friends out on Main Street. There the heavy flakes were falling on the lights strung across Main Street, and the colors glowed on the newly restored glossy buildings.

Nettie looked around at her happy extend family. These were the best moments of her life, and it was exhausting her. She leaned into Nicolas on her right. "I'm going out for a little air."

He smiled, and they held hands. "Okay, Mother."

Her heart swelled to hear those words again from her son, and she passed in front of the man next to Nicolas. "Excuse me."

He smiled and moved his feet, and Nettie smiled back. Startled, she paused for a second, *Caleb*?

She looked back at Nicolas.

They look like twins.

She started down the aisle again. Puzzled, she looked back. *It's only Nicolas.*

Nettie stepped out onto Main Street and took a deep breath to clear her head. A foot of new fallen snow caused a thrill to rush over her. It covered the ground in a thick blanket and topped the glistening Christmas decorations.

Suddenly feeling young again, she laid in the snow on the hill of the church lawn and slowly began moving her arms and legs. She carefully pulled herself to her feet to admire the snow angel she just made.

She laughed remembering making snow angels with Caleb near the old Elkport church.

She walked into the street, her feet leaving small imprints. She pulled her coat and scarf tighter against the brisk night air, admiring the red bells and tinsel draped across the street in perfect arches all the way down Main.

It looks like they go on for eternity. Miki helped make our town a work of art. This is the most joyous night of my life. Everything is right with the world. It's like a drea...

A familiar sound caught her attention—the sound of distant sleigh bells. She stood and turned around, just as it came around the bend.

Old Glory?

It looked like a Currier and Ives lithograph as the sleigh came closer to Nettie. Mesmerized, she didn't move from the middle of the street.

Is that Caleb's dad? I recognize the sleigh and the top hat. But wait. That can't be, he's dead.

She listened to the jingle jangle of bells on the leather straps and the clopping of hooves as the sleigh came closer.

It is Caleb's dad. I recognize the H on the front of the carriage.

She rubbed her eyes trying to focus on what could only be a mirage. But then, a lusty whinny.

Who's pulling the sleigh?

The horse started to nicker and snort and galloped toward Nettie. She grabbed the horse's halter, and they rubbed noses.

"Glory?"

The dappled horse seemed euphoric, and she licked her lips. Her black tail swished, her coat gleaming under the streetlights.

"I know my darling, I love you, too."

Nettie stared intently trying to focus, sure she was seeing Caleb wearing his dad's top hat.

With a huge smile on his face, he jumped out of the sleigh and walked to her.

"Hello, my sweetheart."

He removed his gloves, cupped her face in his large hands, and bent down to kiss her. He remembered the top hat, removed from his head, and set it on Glory's head.

"Here, hold this."

Glory snorted.

Caleb cupped her face and again, bent down to kiss her. Old Glory nosed Caleb closer to Antionette. They lost their balance and laughed at the horse's antics.

Just then the church bells started to ring.

Caleb looked at the belfry. "It's midnight. We have a long way to go."

They both ran to the sleigh and climbed aboard.

"Hold on," he warned. Caleb raised the whip and cracked it in the crisp air. The sleigh seemed to move in slow motion allowing them to take in the scene of Christmas lights, passing under the banners one by one.

They laughed as Caleb made a U-turn and guided the horse back through the banners, only this time the horse ran faster and faster until the sleigh lifted off the ground. It touched down again, but then lifted into the air the second time.

"Hark the Herald Angels Sing" rang from the church as they passed by. Onto the museum and Nettie commented how strange it was to see everything from so high up.

Caleb guided the sleigh for an extra big loop down Main in front of the church, mere feet off the ground where two little girls were standing on the steps.

Jemma shrieked. "It's Santa, there he goes. I just saw Santa! He's weal. Mommy, Mommy!" She jumped up and down.

Navy pointed up. "Mrs. Claus was with him, but there was a horse pulling the sleigh."

"No, they was weindeer. I saw 'em. Wudolph's nose was wed."

They looked at each other for a second and then ran inside yelling, "Mommy, Daddy!"

Congregants were starting to leave church. Two men looked down Main and saw a dark shape in the middle of the street. The men rushed toward the figure, and waved retired Marty to join them. He held up his flashlight as he trounced through the snow..

"It's Nettie," he said softly. He placed his index finger on her neck. "She's gone."

Marty noticed cutter marks down the street. He shined his flashlight on the museum window. The sleigh was gone.

Nettie gone. The sleigh?

Just then, Jemma and Navy ran down the street. They spotted Nettie's snow angel. They flopped down and made some snow angels of their own.

"We saw Santa and Miss Claws—they're weal!" Jemma excitedly shared with Officer Marty.

Marty absently nodded and shined his light on the snow angels. One big one and two small ones.

Nettie?

He walked over to the museum. The front door was open, and there were drag marks on the hard wood floor and across the threshold.

"I'll be. Mrs. Claus was with Santa. Nah. How could that be? I guess that sleigh really was magic. The legend was true."

Jemma and Navy ran down the street. The sound of little rubber boots in the thick snow absorbed into the atmosphere.

"I wonder what Santa brought us?" asked Jemma.

Mom and Dad tried to keep up.

"Girls, slow down!" called their dad.

They ran up the front steps of their house met by porch pillars wrapped in colored Christmas lights and two brightly wrapped gifts.

"He came! He came!" The sisters jumped up and down squealing with delight. They each found one with their own name and tore into the paper.

Breathless, Dad pulled off his hat. "Did you do this?"

Mom's eyes widened. "I didn't! What's going on?"

Mystified, Dad said, "I wish I knew."

Chapter Fifty

CHRISTMAS MORNING everyone gathered at Nettie's. They knew that's how she would want it. Through tears and smiles, they sat around the pine scented tree and opened the presents under the boughs.

Miki noticed some cards on each present, so she picked a box with her name on it.

> Thank you, my dear Miki, for the help on the
> museum and the town. Think of the children
> who will come to learn about their history.
> – Love, Grandma

Inside was a lighted replica she made of the museum with the garret and windmill.

Miki passed out the rest of the cards.

> My dear son Nicolas Emmanuel, here is the German
> church that had such a strong attachment to your
> father and I. Remember my dear boy how much
> your parents loved you. You were wanted and loved.
> I'm so glad I got to finally know you. –Love, Mother

Nick had a small present that was not in the box. It was the leather collar with *Tammy* etched in brass. He began to cry. "Mother. Mother."

Miki read the rest of the cards as each person opened their present.

My Noel, my wish for you is to write and publish you story about Albert. I can't wait to see it in a bookstore. I'm leaving you the Victorian bookstore and $20,000 to publish your book. – Love, Mother

For Hank, I'm leaving you the blacksmith shop since your ancestor was a blacksmith. I'm so proud of you and glad you returned to us. – Love, Mother

For Miki, I am leaving my house where I grew up. Tammy, Glory, and the two trees. And the sleigh. I'll check in on you occasionally like Tammy and Glory watched over me. (And your Uncle Nick.) – Love, Grandma Nettie

For Mary Kaye Bishop Rawley my new daughter, I want you to have the dress shop Victorian house because you are such a fine seamstress. I love the apron you made me. – Love, Nettie

To Beatrice & Peter: Here is my carving of Baby Jesus. To remind us of Christ's love and the love we shared of another little boy so special to both of us! "God so loved the world that he gave his only begotten son. That whoever believeth in him should not perish but have everlasting life." John 3:16

I forgive you and hold no grudge. All that was important is that I got to meet my son and know he was raised with love, that he is a good man and so is my grandson. Thank you both for loving my son. – Love, Nettie

For Nicolas and North, Enjoy your new home. Now you two have a "man cave" to do your art. – Love, Mom, Grandma.

The sleigh followed the highway going east and gently landed on the pavement.

"Much better, Caleb. I like to hear the clopping."

"Are you cold, sweetheart?"

"Well, I was freezing before you picked me up back there. Now I feel warm. I feel like I'm eighteen when I look at you. You should see our son! He's your spitting image."

"I know, isn't it wonderful? Did you name him Emmanuel like we talked about?"

"Yes. I did. But he has a new name now. Nicolas Emmanuel Keller. He's so wonderful. It took so long for me to get to see him, forty-five years." Nettie studied Caleb's face. "I don't want this night to end."

"It won't, hold on. We're going to go down memory lane." Caleb cracked the whip twice in the air.

"Old Glory is beautiful tonight."

The sleigh started to rise.

"Oh, Caleb, not again."

The sleigh kept getting higher.

"Relax."

"It scares me to look down there." Something familiar caught her eye. "What are those lights? Oh, its Elkport…at Christmas. I love how the light through the stained-glass windows of the old German church makes a rainbow in the snow."

"I'll circle back. I love seeing the candles in our windows."

He lowered the sleigh down to Main Street.

Nettie elbowed his ribs. "So, you put up the lights around my yard without me this year?"

They drove past Nettie's house all trimmed in lights.

"I miss Mama and Papa." Nettie looked at the trees in the front yard, and she felt sad remembering that Glory and Tammy were buried under them. Wait. No, they aren't. Tammy barked. She is right next to Nettie and the feeling fleeted. They are both well and happy.

Caleb looked at Tammy and then at Nettie. He said nothing, but a wry smile crossed his lips. He cracked the whip twice in the air, and Glory took them past the shiny new "Entering Elkport" sign.

"So many beautiful lights in Elkport, it's more beautiful than I remember."

"You did that. Don't act so surprised. You always make things better wherever you are."

Nettie smiled. "The church looks so beautiful trimmed with lights, and the Nativity in the front of the church. They've never done that before. Everyone raves about the painting…Caleb, you're going to hit the church, LOOK OUT."

Caleb laughed, cracked the whip twice, and whirled it three times. They bolted straight up the face of the church.

"Wheeeee." Nettie squealed throwing caution to the wind, and she opened her arms. They flew by the ringing belfry.

"I'm starting to have fun with these flying stunts. That was exciting. Let's do it again."

Caleb and Glory acknowledge, and then they left Elkport, Garber, and Osterdock.

Nettie noticed children pointing up at them and chasing them down the street. "You're very good at this, you know."

"I've been practicing for months."

Elkport was out of site, and Nettie thought about the museum door being left open, and the drag marks on the threshold.

She looked behind her, and it made her a little sad that Elkport was gone.

Then she looked at her beau.

"My, you are beautiful, my love." Caleb smiled, and his eyes sparkled.

"Don't be ridiculous, I'm an old lady."

"You have the shine of youth with those chubby pink cheeks."

Nettie touched her face. She was eighteen again.

The bare frozen trees and stubbled corn fields beneath them were sprinkled with twinkling magic as they passed over.

"Why are you here?"

"To get you."

"I can't wait till tomorrow. The whole family is coming over to my house again. I wrapped presents for everyone. And they can finally meet you. I've told them so much about you." She looked at Tammy's panting face and softly petted her white and golden-brown fur.

"Wait, what do you mean 'come to get me.'"

"They sent me."

"Who?"

"Your parents. They figured you would like to see me and your pets first. A sleigh to take you home with Glory, me, and Tammy."

Now Nettie understood. She scanned the scene around her and leaned into Caleb. "Love is a journey, and the journey is timeless."

THE END

$$Epilogue$$

M IKI AND FRANKLIN were married on Easter and soon after she learned that the rabbit had died, (as Grandma Nettie would have termed it.) Linny said he wanted to name the baby Nicolas. Miki asked him what if it's a girl? He said, it's not a girl, I can feel it, it will be a boy.

After their daughter was born on December 23rd, they had a rigorous discussion and decided to name her Niki Antoinette Wimmer as a compromise.

Hank later was admitted to the Blacksmith Union. He was often invited to do demonstrations for school children; they could learn how to make a common nail and take it home for a souvenir.

Noel and Hank were remarried on Easter as well. The two couples had a combined reception at the Barn Community Center. When the bride and groom dance was about to start someone yelled that it was snowing.

"It's *Easter*," moaned nearly everyone in the room.

When they opened the curtains the snow outside transformed the dance room into beautiful winter wonderland.

Miki ran up to the DJ and asked him to play White Christmas.

The two newly married couples ran outside in front of the picture window, and everyone started to clap.

As Noel danced, she was catching snowflakes on her tongue when

Hank pulled her into a long and passionate kiss. A photographer caught the wonder of the moment.

As Bing Crosby crooned their favorite Christmas song, Miki looked up at the sky, "thank you Grandma Nettie. This is the best wedding gift ever! I knew you would come."

The couples go back inside where everyone is singing "White Christmas" and the two couples join in.

Anita and Fanny are walking down Historic Main Street in front of The Barn.

"It's April, enough of this snow," grumbled Fanny.

"Did you hear the couple that bought the old bank building is from San Francisco," tattled Ms. Sniff.

Anita saw Miki and Noel out dancing in the snow. She left her friend and ran up to the two women.

"I want you two to have these." She handed each of them a book. "I don't have much but thought you might enjoy this book about how to have a happy marriage. It's a best seller."

"Thank you so much," said Noel.

"This is so sweet of you Anita," said Miki.

Fanny took Anita's arm, "Merry Christmas, ladies. Come on Anita—we're going to get buried alive out here."

My Dear Readers,

WE HOVER FROZEN in the crisp air as our couple fly on and on, over the Mississippi River and against the background of a huge golden moon. They become a mere black silhouette crossing its face, and thence into a cloud. A flash of light and they are accepted in, never to be seen again in this life. We cannot as mere mortals be allowed to see more; I have already cheated by showing you the beginning of their new journey. Please forgive.

And that dear reader is my first ghost town Christmas story. Hold fast to the ones you love. Have charity to all, and a heart full of gratitude. Merry Christmas to you all, and to all a blessed night!

This is the little German Lutheran church as it stands today. Elkport church built in 1875 is one of two structures that survived a terrible flood in 2004. Residents and members founded an endowment fund to preserve the edifice and history of Elkport. *(Photo taken by Patricia M Boardman)*

In the 1800s Germany was in great turmoil. It was not a country but a collection of smaller kingdoms in a feudal system where the common citizen could not own land. The industrial revolution ended working from home industries which caused a loss of income. With high taxes and mandatory military service young men were forced to leave a country that was in a state of revolution and great instability.

John Schweikert, Wilhemina Trausch or Trandt his first wife where part of an enormous exodus of Germans who came to America for opportunity and freedom. DNA flow charts follow this large settlement of Germans to Dubuque, Clayton and Delaware counties in Iowa. Many people in the Midwest share this common heritage today. There are numerous descendants of these brave pioneers who came to a place where they didn't know the language but worked hard and wove themselves into the fabric of midwestern history.

John arrived in New York in 1844 on the ship St. Nicolas. He fought in the Mexican War and purchased a farm near the Elkport-Garber area. By trade he was a carpenter, and he passed those skills down to his sons. The next generation moved to Dubuque and worked carving elaborate cabinets for phonographs in 1914.

This was the home of the John Schweikert family. It was a barn converted into a house. John was a carpenter and no doubt was put to the test converting this into a house. Sixteen children were raised here by two wives. John's first wife Wilhelmina Trausch (Trandt) died giving birth to my great grandmother Dorothea Charlotte. She was christened in a Lutheran Church in Wisconsin as the Elkport Church was not built until 1875. In the 1950s the last remaining children returned home to try to find their former house. They took their picture in front of it and then went inside where in the attic loft they found their fathers beaver top hat and their mothers spinning wheel wrapped and tucked away after all those years.

Acknowledgements

I would like to thank Richard Paul Evans for starting the authorready.com mentorship. In 2020 decided I wanted to read the book *The Christmas Box* book which has always been one of my favorite Hallmark Hall of Fame movies. After locating a used copy online, I noticed a little button on the top right, "Follow RPE." So, I figured what the heck it could be interesting. A few weeks later I received an email asking me to join his new mentorship authorready.com. So, I thought why not? I had never written a novel before, so I checked it out. It changed my life. Ten months later I had completed a book. This book would not have happened without him. Thanks, Richard.

I'd like to also thank our weekly teacher Debbie Ihler Rasmussen for all her encouragement week by week as the chapters were written. She also helped me with content editing, and I learned a lot from that process. Lola Taylor and graphic artist Maria Levene for the fantastic cover they helped me create. Next, was Kim Autrey my detailed proofreader and Francine Platt, a terrific formatter. You can't lose with a team like this.

I wish to thank my sister Karen Boardman who asks me every day how my book is coming. She always tells me to keep going because she knows I can do it. My brother Arthur (Butch) Boardman who also believes in me. Both are intellectually disabled but their genuine faith and thoughtfulness are always appreciated by me.

I would like to thank my sister Kristine King for all the happy memories in our young years of doing genealogical research together tramping through cemeteries, ghost towns and county courthouses. They were and still are my happiest memories with her.

I couldn't forget my children, Alicia DeVey, April Borra, Daniel Haines, and Crystal Edwards and my eight grandkids. I love that we all like to face our fears and do new things to challenge ourselves.

And my roommate Wyvanna Hood who watched my dog and my sister so I could go to Utah to Richards seminar a year ago. Then to the Authors Timepiece Ranch Retreat in June. And lastly to Iowa to network with people and photograph places I have written about in this book. I couldn't have done this without her.

Lastly, my dog Gromit a miniature black and tan dachshund. He mentioned to me one late night, that he thought there needed to be a dog companion in the story. I looked at him and said, "You're right!" That's my little buddy!

About the Author

Patricia M Boardman is genealogist, writer, historian and actress.

A lifelong genealogist she turned to history to understand the story of her ancestors once the documents revealed all they could. Her passion covers many aspects of history. "Under every tombstone is a story" is her motto. She is from Dubuque, Iowa but has lived in Southern California for the last 37 years.

Patricia created the Pint-Size Pioneer Program for elementary school children to teach history and good citizenship. She served on the board of the Santa Ana Historical Preservation Society where she wrote, directed several historic cemetery tours educate the public. She also published a book for the Orange County Cemetery District called *Remember Me: Mini-biographies of Pioneers Buried in the Santa Ana Cemetery*—a self-guided historic tour of the Santa Ana Cemetery with map.

The author is a mother of four and grandmother of eight.